CLAIMED

SINS OF THE SIGMA

PREQUEL NOVELLA

A DARK COLLEGE ROMANCE

THE ORIGIN OF KIEREN & MONROE

SUMMER ROBERT

Published by Silly J Media LLC

Cover design and © by Seventhstar Art.

Mask Illustration by Seventhstar Art; Copyright Owner: Silly J Media LLC.

Developmental and Copy Editing by Brandy Gibson.

CONTENT WARNING: *Claimed* and the *Sins of the Sigma* series in general contains some themes that may be distressing to readers, including narcissism, references to Narcissistic Personality Disorder (NPD), memories of neglect and abuse from a narcissistic parent, Borderline Personality Disorder (BPD), gaslighting, physical abuse, emotional manipulation, obsession with and desire to possess another human, stalking, drug and alcohol use.

Most importantly, as someone who has had personal, childhood experiences with NPD and BPD, please heed the following content warning: *If you have been in a relationship with a narcissist, have a close family member, including a parent(s) who is a narcissist, or have difficulty reading about narcissistic behavior, please consider your mental health before reading this book and series.* Although there are moments of redemption and scenes of triumph throughout this series, it does not come full circle for the heroine Monroe until the last book. Writing this series was both cathartic, heartbreaking, and redeeming, and my wish for anyone reading this series is to feel the same.

SEXUAL CONTENT: This novella contains detailed and explicit two-person sex scenes that include elements of degradation, biting, bondage, captive prisoner role play, pain play, primal play, use of BDSM toys and other BDSM elements.

This book is intended for mature, adult audiences only. Please read with caution.

READER NOTE: *Claimed* is the prequel to *Caged* and the origin point for the rest of the *Sins of the Sigma* series. This novella covers the events that unfolded between Kieren Hunt and his obsession, Monroe Campbell, during their freshman year at Dornell University, including how they met. *Claimed* covers critical moments in time and is not meant to be a continuous story of their entire freshman year. This novella ends with a *To Be Continued* and does not end with a *Happily Ever After.*

You do not need to read *Claimed* before reading *Caged.* In fact, this novella is best read between Books 1 and 2 of the series. You may find that this novella provides a helpful reference point to better understand the mental states of both Kieren and Monroe. Readers will also meet characters in *Claimed* that play a larger role later in the series, including Knox Sterling and Reid Carver.

BLURB: CLAIMED

Claimed,
Prequel Novella to the
Sins of the Sigma Series:

A private school elitist with a dark side.
An insecure outsider from humble beginnings.
A chance encounter that would change the course of their lives forever.

Both incoming freshmen at Dornell University, Kieren Hunt is inexplicably drawn to Monroe Campbell like a moth to a flame, and what starts as a budding infatuation quickly morphs into possessive obsession. She's everything he's not - no prestige, no wealth, a nobody - yet exactly what his controlling dominance craves. A blank canvas to mold.

He claimed her. He trained her. She would be his perfect pet.

It was destiny sealed with desire. It was obsession disguised as love.

It was the beginning of the end: the ill-fated origin of Kieren and Monroe.

SINS OF THE SIGMA SERIES OVERVIEW

Important Information About the Series

Sins of the Sigma is a dark and suspenseful secret society romance series with elements of mystery, revenge, betrayal, power, greed, carnal desires, obsession, and love. This four-book series and prequel novella follow a fluid group of villains, vigilantes, and antiheroes on their quest for greatness, legacy, understanding, and justice.

Throughout the series, enemies will become lovers, lovers will become enemies, past lovers will get a second chance, and above all else, blood will be spilled. What starts as the resurrection of Sigma fraternity's secret traditions at Dornell University unfolds into a sinister web of boundless greed and unchecked fanaticism with a mystery that doesn't come full circle until the last book.

Great power demands sacrifice, after all. You must give in order to get.

The following is helpful to know when reading the series:

Caged (Book 1) and *Collared* (Book 2) follow the same set of characters and take place during the same time period at college. Books 1 and 2 are not a duet in the traditional sense but can be considered a 'cluster'.

Carved (Book 3) and *Crossed* (Book 4) follow new characters (although some may be familiar but just look a little different) and take place in the near future after the conclusion of Book 2. As is the case for the first two books, the last two books are not a traditional duet but can be considered a 'cluster'.

Each book has a different Main Male Character of focus, although many characters crossover into multiple books throughout the series. Books 2, 3, and 4 do end with a happily ever after.

Note: Other than the prequel, the series is meant to be read in order.

TENTATIVE SERIES RELEASE DATES

Caged
A Dark Secret Society Revenge Romance
(Book #1, November 2025)

Claimed
A Dark College Romance Novella
(Prequel, February 2026)

Collared
A Dark Secret Society Second Chance Romance
(Book #2, Expected Release April 2026)

Carved
A Dark Secret Society Workplace Romance
(Book #3, Expected Release October 2026)

Crossed
A Dark Secret Society, Enemies to Lovers, Second Chance Romance

(Book #4, Expected Release H1 2027)

ALSO BY SUMMER ROBERT

The Good Hurt Series

Good Hurt

(Book #1, a Dark College Romance)

Splinter

(Book #2, a Dark College Romance)

Salvation

(Book #3, a Dark College Romance)

To all my sweet puppies who just want to be loved.

This series will ruin you.

Buckle up because this is only the beginning.

1
KIEREN

Beginning of Freshman Year,
Dornell University

The only interesting thing worth watching at this pathetic return to campus barbecue event is the glistening bead of sweat slowly descending her inner thigh. It clings to her summer-tanned skin, and every few seconds, advances another inch or two before pausing, waiting, gathering steam, and then continuing. I wonder if she can feel the tickle of it as it rolls farther down, now almost to her knee. If she notices, she makes no move to wipe it away. Maybe she likes it – the feeling of wet heat pooling at her base to the point of overflowing. I wonder what my finger might find if I tucked it beneath her short white skirt. Her soft pussy would no doubt be scorching to the touch.

As if in answer, my pointer finger pulses in anticipation, growing hot as if it's already inside her. My dick swells against my shorts, and I right myself, shaking off the trance. I look around, swallowing the saliva now threatening to choke me, to see if anyone has noticed the growing tent below my waistband.

The late summer heat in upstate New York is insufferable at this time of day. Stifling humidity bears down on those congregated in the backyard of Sigma for the annual welcome back party. It's an open event, a chance for existing members to scout incoming students for talent and potential. Men, most hardly past pubescent, stand around in pit-stained salmon or navy-blue polo shirts, because picking a shirt of a different color obviously requires too many fucking brain cells. I inwardly sneer at their attempts to converse with the latest crop of freshmen women. Their hollow chit-chat grates against my skin, and I resist the urge to suckerpunch the nearest dickbag in the throat.

The sausage-to-bun ratio at this barbecue is pitiful. Christ, I've never seen such riffraff. I wouldn't be surprised if every dumbass with a dick from the arriving class is here. Ninety percent of these fuckers won't be given a second look by The Brotherhood, let alone be invited to pledge.

But then again, Sigma has grown soft, weakened by the current crop of brothers allowed to join after Dornell reinstated the fraternity's charter six years ago. Sigma was once infamous under the reign of those who understood that brutality was necessary for greatness, but that was a long time ago.

My grandfather, a Sigma alumnus and legend in his day, would share stories at the holiday table of a Sigma unchecked by university ethics bullshit. Pledges would be hazed within an inch of their lives to prove worthiness. Servitude to The Brotherhood trumped all else. Sigma's darker side – a more deviant and secretive Sigma I'm told – flourished, and brothers were revered on campus as untouchable gods, or so my grandfather would whisper to me after one too many pours of single malt Scotch. We're quite similar, my grandfather and I, and although he's never divulged much about his own bedroom proclivities, I suspect I have him to thank for my... *desires.*

My feckless father is also a Sigma alumnus, and much to his chagrin, he knows both my ruthlessness and calculated ingenuity are also inherited gifts from my grandfather, *not him*; natural gifts he desperately wishes he had but clearly never received. His inferiority to his own son plagues him like an untreatable cancer, although he'll never admit it aloud, but I know his jealousy is there. His relentless scrutiny and belittling of me, or if I'm lucky, his blatant disregard, are admission enough.

What a fucking joke. My father may have his country club buddies fooled, but not me. I know he's nothing more than a worthless, spineless heir, mediocre at best. My grandfather knows it, too. But despite this unspoken truth, my father does, and always has, thought highly of himself, externally undeterred by the obviousness of his own shortcomings. Convinced he's on par with the likes of Fortune 50 CEOs, British and European nobility; hell, even the President of the United States.

He and I both know our family would be nowhere if it weren't for the selfless labors of my grandfather, and my father has been content to shamelessly ride his coattails of success, greedy and self-entitled, for his entire adult life. I fear, at some point, his complacency will catch up to him, but hopefully, when that day comes, I'll already be at the helm of our family's fortune and can coerce my father into early retirement. But if not, I'm sure my father will relegate me to clean-up crew, knowing I have the fortitude to tackle even the most arduous and unethical of tasks. He's always known I have a propensity for the morally ambiguous, which is why I think he lets half the shit I do slide. I might be useful to you one day, after all, Father.

To his credit, he's not wrong. I do have a knack for *fixing things*, just like I plan to fix this fucking disgrace of a fraternity that is Sigma. The Sigma empire of days past was untouchable. Powerful. This version of Sigma, swarming with pussy-ass motherfuckers, I can barely stomach.

I tear away from my thoughts of disdain for those standing around me and return to my sweaty queen.

Pretty.

So fucking pretty.

She stands awkwardly at the edge of the crowd, her back to me as it has been for several minutes. The plastic cup filled with piss-tasting keg beer is clutched between her palms. She sips at it as she scans the towering maple trees that rim the lawn behind Sigma house, pretending, I assume, to admire the foliage instead of forcing herself into conversation with strangers. Can't say I blame her in this current environment.

Curiosity nags at me until my feet begin to move in her direction. Blonde hair falls past her shoulders in limp waves that beg for a breeze. Judging by the crown of her head, it's not her natural hair color, but the way blonde strands blend seamlessly into darker ones reminds me of girls who attended my private high school.

Yet I don't know her.

"Admiring the leaves?" I ask upon silent approach.

She startles, and I force back a grin. Dark oval sunglasses turn in my direction. Her mouth quirks, unsure if she should be receptive or alarmed. I suppose I do have a rather menacing look about me, towering over her by at least half a foot, but my imposing dominance has always been part of my charm.

"Umm, yeah, I guess," she responds, caught off-guard, and dare I say, *nervous*.

Shy. Perfect. "I'm Kieren," I offer, extending a hand.

"Monroe," she responds as she grasps my outstretched hand in greeting.

Her palm is hot and slightly damp to the touch, but *fuck*, her skin is so goddamn smooth, I want to lick it, taste it.

"You a freshman?" I ask, curtailing my wanton thoughts. Forcing my limbs into a casual stance takes considerable effort. My eyelids flare with an instinctual, primal intensity, and I hear that prescient voice in my head scream at me to calm the fuck down. *For fuck's sake, Kieren, you* just *met this woman. You'll scare her, and you don't want to scare this one.*

The voice is right, and I take an unnoticeable, nonchalant step back.

She nods as if none the wiser. "Yes. You?"

My gaze dips from her sunglasses down to her mouth. Her berry-tinted lips are full but not pouty; her defined Cupid's bow no doubt would have served as a muse for Roman sculptors should she have been alive during such ancient times. *Beautiful.*

"Regrettably," I answer, hypnotized by those fucking lips.

This earns a chiding laugh, snapping me from my fixation. "Why regrettably?"

I shrug, certain we're on the same page, and then gesture to the lawn behind me, packed with bodies. "Because of shit like this. It all feels so tiresome, doesn't it? Being forced into conversation with morons you'll likely never see again and the charade of having to give a shit."

"Wow. Mr. Friendly," she scoffs. Her raised eyebrows flare above her black sunglasses, and I sense her body stiffen, seconds from pulling away.

Realizing she didn't interpret my answer as the pretentious joke I had intended, I scramble for the right words to better explain myself. "No, I just mean that coming from where we come from, we already know anyone worth knowing."

"Jesus! It just gets worse!" she declares to no one, turning away.

Oh, is she not... one of us? Is she actually offended?

"What do you mean?" I feign, softening my tone to surprised confusion.

Her pause is barely perceptible, but I notice. "Nothing. I was joking," she quips. I'm sure she thinks she's given me a sassy response, but I can tell by the way she now inadvertently chews at the inside of her lower lip that I've grazed a nerve.

Curious. I decide to keep going.

"Where'd you go to high school?" I ask.

"Nowhere you've heard of," she responds. Her body remains half-turned away from me, but with no one nearby to pull into our conversation, she's trapped.

"Try me," I press, doing my best to keep my tone lighthearted.

When she doesn't answer, I rattle off names of private high schools across the U.S.: "Riverdale, Groton, Commonwealth?" She shakes her head. "Harvard-Westlake?" I ask, throwing out a school on the West Coast.

"I didn't go to private school," she interjects with a frustrated huff. "I grew up on Long Island. Not the trust fund side of Long Island, but working-class Long Island. Then I moved to Ohio when I was twelve."

A chip on her shoulder, or is it insecurity? This explains her uncomfortable stance.

"Ohio?" I ask, shocked, because honestly, I am. "You don't strike me as someone from the Midwest."

"I only lived there for six years," she corrects.

"But your teenage years are the most formative," I counter.

"Okay, Andover," she mocks with newfound vigor. Now I'm getting somewhere.

"Is it that obvious?" I jest, because I know between my cliché old-money aesthetic and Rolex on my wrist, I'm practically a walking brochure.

"Just... look at you," she sneers, not picking up on my self-deprecating sarcasm.

An unintentionally smug smile tugs at the corners of my mouth. "If I didn't know better, I'd think you were complimenting me."

"Ha!" she blurts. "Not quite."

I can't tell if she's intrigued and flirting with me or annoyed.

"Where on Long Island, did you say?" I ask.

"Hicksville and I didn't."

Oh, she's most definitely annoyed. The grin that spreads across my face is nearly feral I'm sure.

"Huh. Hicksville and Ohio," I repeat, unable to help myself. "I must say, you hide it well."

"Oh my God, okay, I've got to..."

She abruptly pivots to walk away, and I grab her wrist on impulse. Forceful. Too forceful. She stops, but I can feel her muscles tense under my palm in a way that tells me the firmness of my touch is not appreciated. *Not yet, anyway.*

"Wait," I say, adjusting my strategy. "I think we got off on the wrong foot." Taking a deep breath and plastering a smile on my face that I hope is friendly, I continue. "Let's start over," I begin, releasing my grip. She lets her arm drop but gives me what I can only assume is a death glare behind those infuriatingly opaque sunglasses.

"Hi, I'm Kieren Hunt." For good measure, I yield a placating dip of my chin, even though I am wholly unaffected by her attitude. "I'm a freshman poli-sci major with a minor in economics. I grew up in Connecticut, and yes, I went to Andover."

She huffs an indignant *'I knew it'* laugh as I make a show of patiently waiting for her reintroduction.

"You already know my name," she grumbles.

"Not your last name," I politely correct.

"Campbell," she says cautiously, like she might regret sharing this information later, and I can promise that she most certainly will. "I'm a computer science major. I already told you where I grew up, and I went to a no-name public high school."

"CS?" I all but gasp. I want to ask how it's possible that a girl from Hicksville who attended a no-name public high school in Ohio got accepted as a computer science major at Dornell University. But, I can tell she's grown unamused with my antics, and sensing her thinning patience, I playfully ask, "Why would you do that to yourself?"

A strange pause follows my question as I watch her brows knit together. "Do you know that person?"

"Who?" I ask, turning to follow her line of sight.

Dammit.

"The brunette in the jean shorts and black tank top glaring daggers at us?"

"Oh, yeah, that's my ex," I say nonchalantly, running a hand through my hair as I turn back around. *Fuck.* Calling Tierney my ex is a stretch, but Monroe, whom I barely know and have already managed to piss off, doesn't need to know the truth.

"Back to my question," I say to redirect her attention. "What made you want to be a CS major?"

"Ha, honestly, I don't know," she answers, huffing a laugh at her own decision. "I suppose I like pain," she shrugs earnestly, *innocently*, and I swear to fuck I feel my dick twitch.

"Is that so?" I purr, raising an eyebrow at what must have been a flirtatious remark on her part. Finally, this conversation is back on track.

"What dorm are you in?" she asks, ignoring my advance. *Such a tease.* Fine, I'll play along.

"Mews. You?"

"RBG."

"Oh, nice. My buddy is in RBG. What room?" I lightly probe, careful to sound impassive.

"Three twenty-six," she answers.

"Three twenty-six," I repeat. "Interesting." Although there is nothing interesting about her room number; a slip on my part.

"What's his name?" she asks.

"Who?" I ask like a moron.

"*Your friend,*" she sneers, like it should be obvious, and frankly, it is obvious, but victory is mine, you gorgeous creature, and now I know where you live.

"Oh. Not important," I say, waving off the question. I could keep the lie going, but why bother? "Do you want to get out of here?" I ask hastily.

She physically takes a step back, and I'm genuinely perplexed by her sudden change in countenance. This was all going so well, I thought. Textbook, even.

"Wow. Bold," she remarks, stunned.

"Why is that bold?" I criticize, frowning. Truly, I don't understand this woman. One minute, she's flirting with me, the next minute, she's gawking at me as if I said something audaciously uncouth.

"If you want to continue drinking warm keg beer and making small talk with idiots, then by all means, stay," I retort with a judgmental flip of my hand, irked to have misinterpreted the situation. Immediately, though, I regret my rash comment, because a mocking, full-toothed smile stretches wide across her face, one of manic delight that would cause even the most callous of villains to beg for absolution.

"No thanks," she states in finality, like I'm a pitiful and disgusting slob propositioning her at a bar.

She sidesteps me in two strides, without so much as a parting glance in my direction. Awestruck by her rejection, I wordlessly turn to watch her go, marking her flawless backside as she weaves through the throngs of bodies. Goddamn, she is gorgeous. My jaw ticks as I watch the lingering stares of lesser men trail her perfect form. My fingers flex and relax to temper the tingling, jealous rage skating up my arms, down my torso, my legs... Failure swirls in my head, roiling with inexplicable need and insatiable hunger.

Who *is* this girl?

Monroe.

I commit those lips to memory; *those perfect goddamn lips.*

Well, I don't think so, *Monroe.*

You may think you're done with me, *but you'd be wrong,* because nobody walks away from Kieren Hunt.

2
MONROE

G*et the fuck out of my way,* I think as I glare at each oversized frat boy who stands between me and finding a way out of this shithole. Of all the self-entitled twats I've met since I set foot on this campus, Kieren – whatever-the-fuck he said his last name was – tops them by a mile.

Broad shoulders part, and gawking eyes I don't care to meet track me as I pass. I skirt around their hulking frames like a mouse scurrying through a maze. Their objectifying looks make my skin crawl with disgust. I don't know why I thought things would be different once I got to Dornell – once I got away from the high school boys who only wanted a hole to fuck.

Even my crooked stepdad's cronies behaved better. Although, I did hear my stepdad threaten them on numerous occasions to stay the hell away from me if they wanted to keep their balls intact.

Whatever. Fuck my loser stepdad for getting my mom involved in his racketeering bullshit, and fuck my mom for being so goddamn imbecilic. I wonder when she's going to call me again. It's been a few months, and usually, she runs out of money by now.

"Where is the door?" I ask the first person I see. Getting inside from the back lawn was easy, but now I have to figure out how to get out of here. Everything inside the fraternity looks the same: dark wood tables, dark wood chairs, dark brown leather furniture that looks like it's been shat on, puked on, and stabbed, an ominous fireplace, another ominous fireplace, twisting stairs leading everywhere and yet nowhere at the same time.

When I arrived, I blindly followed the girls I had come with through the zigzagging hallways until we reached double doors that opened onto a slender back porch and sprawling yard. I followed them out to the kegs, queued to get a beer, turned around, and they were gone. I managed small talk with zit-faced guys until I could no longer suffer through another conversation about private high schools, and then I met Kieren. *Fucking asshole Kieren.*

"Leaving so soon? The party just started," the guy comments without answering my question.

"And yet I've already had enough," I retort.

The way he scoffs tells me these *'men'*, if they can be called that, don't get told *'no'* often. Especially not by women.

"That way," he gestures vaguely. He's already begun walking away, so I'm left with little choice but to follow his irritatingly unhelpful directions.

Female voices sound nearby, and I follow the noise. The hallway opens into a massive room, decorated like a Gothic castle. I glance up at the prominent wooden beams covered with strange carvings that line the vaulted ceiling and trace their lines down to the opposite wall. Decorative patterns are also carved into the massive floor-to-ceiling support beams.

More worn brown leather furniture is neatly arranged in the center of the room, giving an undeserved first impression of civility.

Girls wearing clothes bearing designer logos stand in the foyer just inside the ornate, oversized front doors, their faces clad with looks of eager excitement. I overhear the guy on bouncer duty at the door explaining the history of Sigma. "The oldest fraternity on campus," he proclaims with pride as I slip past. Why do the girls look so enthralled? I want to tell them that this party, and frankly, this fraternity, is not fun, and to not waste their time.

I take out my phone once I'm out of sight. I have no idea where I am or how to get back to my dorm. *Thirty minutes*, I sigh to myself. It didn't feel like thirty minutes on the walk here, but I suppose I'll need to get used to walking everywhere. My grandmother let me drive her beat-up Chevy Malibu to Dornell, but I don't trust that thing on these hills. That car is older than I am, but somehow, it's still kicking. Parking also seems to be problematic on campus. I tried to find parking near the building that houses the Registrar's Office when I arrived, but after twenty minutes of circling, I gave up and drove back to my dorm.

Beads of sweat run down the small of my back as I trudge up the endless incline back to North Campus. My skin is uncomfortably sticky from the humidity. Despite the laughably pretentious conversation I just had with Kieren, all I can focus on while I walk is how horrendous my initial interactions with my roommate have been. I pray she isn't there when I get back. For starters, it took me three trips to unload my belongings from my car. It somehow took her, her parents, and her brother all fucking day.

Initially, I was amazed at the generous space of the double room, but it quickly began to feel claustrophobic once she arrived. Her things spilled over every speck of available space, and she was so goddamn unfriendly. I get it – I'm sure on the surface I look like a Midwest cheerleader, and she is the antithesis of my vibe. But that's fine! Why can't we simply be civil to each other? We don't have to be best friends.

And I understand she loves heavy metal music, but would it be too much to ask for her to wear headphones?

The answer is apparently yes, it is too much to ask, because when I did, she laughed at me and said, "Can't you wear earplugs?"

I've only been on campus for three days, and I'm miserable. I feel unwelcome in my own space. How am I going to live with this person for an entire school year? I need to figure out how to switch rooms and do so immediately.

A car horn honks, and I jolt but keep walking.

I whirl around at the second honk.

You have got to be kidding me.

"Need a ride?"

3
MONROE

"Are you serious?" I shout, scowling at Kieren from the sidewalk.

"I'm headed back to the dorms," he hollers. "Get in."

"I already told you, no thanks!" I yell and turn away to continue my trek. Jesus, this man is dogged to the point of creepy.

Another car has pulled to a stop behind Kieren's black BMW and honks angrily at him to move.

"It's just a ride!" he yells in a vain attempt to convince me of his innocent intentions. "Besides, it's sweltering and you look dehydrated."

The aggravated white Volkswagen is unrelenting, not that the trust fund kid staring at me seems to care at all. I, however, feel anxious over a situation I didn't cause.

"Monroe, it's just a ride, I promise!" he yells again.

I shoot him a warning glare, and against my better judgment, because I am wearily overheated, cave. "Fine," I huff and stomp over to his car. I make sure he can see the threat on my face when I climb inside.

As soon as I pull the door closed, icy air conditioning blasts my face, and I wish I weren't so relieved.

"Better, right?" he asks with a smirk as he shifts the transmission into drive.

"Did you follow me?" I ask with a suspicious side-eye.

"No, but the barbecue did get infinitely more boring after you stormed off."

"I stormed off because you were being a dick."

"Well, I am a dick. You should probably get used to it," he grins without taking his eyes off the road ahead. I huff out a laugh and lean my head back. Perhaps I mistook his dry humor for pompous. His rich brown irises twinkle with a glimmer I can see even though he's not looking directly at me, and that infuriating dimple on the right side of his mouth almost makes him appear endearing.

Monroe, what the fuck is wrong with you? I scold myself. Someone tell me why I got into a car with this lunatic I barely know. Yes, he's tall. Yes, he's frustratingly attractive. Yes, he looks exactly like the type of guy I would go for, with his dark hair and angular jawline, but didn't I tell myself I need to make better choices? I'm pretty sure those were the exact words I uttered aloud as I watched the image of my frail, hunched grandmother grow smaller and smaller in my rearview mirror.

"I won't be like Mom. I'll do better, Grandma. I promise."

And, fuck. Here I am, barely seventy-two hours into this adventure, breaking that promise.

"I'm kidding! *Relax,*" he chastises when I don't respond. "It's called humor, Monroe. Do they not have a sense of humor in Ohio?"

"Do you really think you're funny?" I snip. "Because I'm not laughing."

He glances over at me with another grin. "You think I'm funny. Admit it."

"I think you're annoying," I retort.

A cocky roll of his eyes has him focused back on the road as he shifts the car into a different gear. The way his body fills the seat as he drives the twisting campus road with ease, commanding but casual, oozing confidence, is enthralling and *fuck*, strangely comforting.

"You're going to regret that manual transmission on these hills once it starts to snow," I say, watching him shift gears again. I don't know why I find his vehicular mastery captivating. It's just a fucking car. But choosing this option is like choosing the stairs instead of an elevator to get to the top floor of a skyscraper simply because you can – *look at me going against the grain instead of following the plebian masses.* Predictably elitist yet so goddamn beguiling.

"So my parents tell me," he responds flatly.

"Are they still here?" I ask.

"No. They didn't help me move in. Far too busy with their own shit. But, they're both alumni, so they're familiar with the campus."

"I'm sorry," I offer, although I can't tell if he is upset or indifferent.

He shrugs. "My mom would just be up my ass the whole time if she were here, and my dad would probably be on his phone working. It's better this way."

"What about your parents?" he asks, looking over at me as he keeps one hand on the steering wheel and the other on the stick shift.

I swallow uncomfortably, unsure if I'm ready to share my upbringing with a man I barely know, whose childhood could not be more different from my own. But, fuck it, once I get out of this car, I likely won't see Kieren again, and I might as well practice reciting my cringeworthy background since it seems that's all anyone at this school cares to know.

"My mom is in prison. My grandma, whom I lived with in Ohio, is too old to make the trip, and my biological father hasn't been around since I was three."

"Oh. Shit," he says, visibly taken aback. My face flushes with shame. Dammit, I've made things awkward.

"Sorry, I don't know why I just said all that," I say with a slight chuckle to lessen the discomfort of my overshare. "I usually don't air my family drama to strangers."

My gaze falters to my clasped hands, clammy with embarrassment, as I rest them in my lap.

"I'm hardly a stranger," he corrects with gentle playfulness. Is he flirting, or simply trying to make me feel less uncomfortable? Either way, a timid glance in his direction, at his earnest expression, soothes my nerves.

"I barely know you, Kieren. You're a stranger," I explain pragmatically. If this *is* his attempt at an olive branch, I don't want to sound snide.

"An hour ago, we were strangers. But now, I'd say we're two people having a moment," he says, matching my matter-of-fact tone.

"We're having *a moment*?" I ask, cynically raising my eyebrows.

"Are we not? We had a little bonding session just now, don't you think? Both of us, with our absent, shitty parents."

I scoff a clipped laugh. "Yeah, but your mom isn't incarcerated and your dad isn't a deadbeat," I say. "That isn't the same degree of shitty."

"Are you trying to make this into a competition about whose parents are the shittiest, Monroe? Because I have more stories," he grins in challenge as he pulls into a parking lot behind a building I recognize as my dorm. I linger on the way his voice sounds when he says my name, even though I know it's a foolish indulgence.

Somewhere in these rows of luxury cars sits my beat-up Chevy Malibu, wedged between a brand-new Mercedes sedan and a Range Rover. Maybe I should pretend I don't have a car, so I don't have to subject myself to the inevitable humiliation I'll feel when asked if I drive a 3 Series or a 4 Series, because, surprise, it's neither.

"Thanks for the ride," I say when Kieren idles to a stop. I reach for the door handle when his fingers delicately skim my left forearm.

"Take my number," he offers, like he can sense my apprehension as I glare at the place where his skin connects with mine. "You know, if you need anything or whatever. I'm sorry to hear about your parents. I'm sure it can't be easy to start college at a school like Dornell without anyone."

Is my abandonment and hardship *that* obvious? That I'm woefully alone in this endeavor, in life, to the point where this arrogant brat feels like I need his philanthropy? My chest tightens with both indignation and insecurity. All the fears I had about coming to this school have started to ring true.

The car interior feels like it has grown ten degrees hotter in the last five seconds, dizzying and claustrophobic. I need to get the fuck out of here, *now,* before my composure melts into a pool of suffocating self-doubt.

"Umm. Sure," I say, flustered, as I fish my phone from my purse.

My fingers quiver with the beginnings of an anxiety attack as he rattles off his number. I'm too triggered to type, so I pretend to save his number.

"Got it. See you around," I say as I open the passenger door and step out of his car on unsteady legs. My hand is shaking as I feebly push the door closed. I doubt it latched, but I don't look back to make sure. I hightail it to the back entrance of my dorm building and wonder if he noticed how unnerved I was getting out of his car. More embarrassment claws at my throat when I dwell on the thought that he probably did notice and now thinks I'm even more of a misfit mess.

Why did I tell him about my parents? *Seriously, why?* I hardly share those details, and certainly not with someone I've just met. What was it about his scant bit of kindness that made me want to open up?

Maybe it was because his offer of a ride, his insistence that I should stop walking uphill in the heat, was the first bit of care anyone had shown me since setting foot on Dornell's campus. Yes, it was a bit alarming that he followed me, although maybe he honestly didn't intend to follow me, and was simply taking the most direct driving route between the fraternity and North Campus, as he claimed.

My mind clings to our conversation, the most normal conversation I've had yet, which is a disconcerting thought, as I round the corner and immediately hear her metal music blasting from the far end of the hallway. *I can't do this*, not right now in my precarious mental state, so I abruptly detour to the nearest women's restroom.

My fingers curl around the edge of the sink as I hold my own gaze in the mirror.

Tears pool along my lower lash line. I was prepared to feel out of place. I was ready to feel less-than when I arrived, knowing most students are bankrolled by their wealthy parents and not struggling to survive on university and federal grants like me.

I worked two fucking jobs this summer just to afford a decent wardrobe and blonde highlights in the hope that both would help me fit in with the rest of the students. What financial aid didn't cover, student loans did, but not without fucking me in the ass with their obscene interest rates first. I'll be shackled with debt for the next thirty years of my life. This education better be worth it, because I cannot go back to a life of poverty. After graduation and four years of subjecting myself to what I'm sure will be academic torture to obtain my engineering degree, I'd better land a tech job with a fat paycheck, move out to San Francisco, and start a new life where I never have to deal with the demon who is my fucking mother ever again.

I grimace at the thought of my mother, exhaling a long breath through my nose. She's been behind bars for six years, yet it feels like I can't escape her. The constant guilt, the nagging presence of her disapproval, the need to criticize every decision I make down to my goddamn hair color, refuses to go the fuck away. *Fuck!* I scream inside my head.

You are stronger than this, Monroe, I scold myself. A tear rolls down my cheek, but I don't break my stare, nor do I lift a hand to wipe it away as my teeth grind together.

You are better than this.

"Are you okay?" I startle at the question. Searing heat ripples across every inch of my skin, and I see my face in the mirror turn crimson. I thought I was alone. The realization that someone else witnessed my complete meltdown is mortifying, and I can't even flee to the safe seclusion of my own dorm room because my hell-worshipping roommate's in there and she's terrifying.

Talking myself down from my ledge of self-loathing, I manage enough poise to apologize for whatever disturbing scene this innocent bystander observed.

"Sorry. I didn't think anyone else was in here," I offer.

I recognize the girl instantly – the gorgeous one with the striking, deep brunette hair that falls in glossy waves down the middle of her back. She's in a room at the opposite end of my hall. I noticed her when she moved in with her parents. In fact, it was hard not to notice her. She could be a model, yet she's here at Dornell, and I just know if I asked her where she goes to get her hair to look like that, she would tell me she's never gone to the salon for more than a trim.

I meet her curious eyes in the mirror. Her irises are pristine, rich brown saucers floating between smoldering, black lashes, a far cry from my eyes, now irritated and red from tears.

"I'm fine," I manage, trying not to gawk at her flawless, tanned olive skin.

"You sure? I know it's a lot. Leaving home," she offers.

It's not that, I want to say. I don't mourn the home I left. I mourn never having a real home to leave. Every other student moved in with the help of their parents, who schlepped and carried and fussed. Every other student brought things *from home* to remind them of the comfort and family they left behind. Every other student calls their parents to share updates and *check in*.

My mom only calls me from prison when she wants me to ask Grandma to put more money in her commissary account, and the fucked-up part about this request is I tell her I'll ask, and then just put the money in myself. I suppose that's why I worked a part-time job all throughout high school. As my legal guardian, my grandma helped me get a Minor Work Permit and open a checking account at our local bank.

There was no need to burden her with my mom's selfishness, not when she barely had enough money in savings to cover her bills and put food on the table for us both. I was the financial curveball she didn't anticipate in her golden years, but she never complained. It's not like my mom cares where the money comes from; only that she gets enough to buy her cigarettes or whatever the hell she claims she needs to survive.

God, do I hate that woman, yet every few months when she

calls, I can't fucking help myself, and send her money like she might one day wake up and give a shit.

"Yeah, it's a lot," I concede to the girl who looks at me with genuine concern and compassion. I've already overshared with one stranger today, no need to make it two.

"I'm Gabriella," she says, extending her hand. "But everyone calls me Gabi."

"Monroe," I respond, clasping her hand in mine.

"Are you in the room with...," she pauses. "Sorry," she says, "I don't know how to say this without sounding mean."

"The asshole who walks around like she hates everybody?" I say for her.

"Yes," Gabi nods slowly.

"Yep. Unfortunately. She's my roommate."

"How's that going?"

"About as good as you might expect."

"I've said 'hi' to her in the hallway numerous times, and she doesn't respond. Like, literally doesn't even acknowledge me. I thought maybe she might have a hearing disability, especially with how loud she blasts her music. Oh, I just assumed the metal music was her taste, which is totally rude because I'm completely stereotyping."

"You're not being rude," I say. "She's rude. I don't know what her problem is, or what I did to deserve her wrath, but she's been a jerk since minute one. The second her parents left, full send with the assholery. I don't know," I shrug.

"What are you going to do? Are you going to transfer rooms?"

"Definitely," I say. "As soon as possible. I don't know how the room transfer thing works, though, or how quickly it can happen."

"It's an application process. You can apply on the first day of classes," she answers. "I looked it up when I moved in because I'm in a double, but my roommate has yet to arrive."

"Wow, you have double all to yourself?" I stammer. "How lucky!"

"Honestly, it's giving me such anxiety. I'm scared someone... not so great will move in mid-semester and I'll be fucked."

Within the same breath she shouts, "Monroe!" she exclaims, eyes wide with glee. "Switch to my room!"

My heart beats wildly in my chest at the prospect, even though I don't know this girl, but compared to the nightmare who is my current roommate, Gabi seems like a dream.

"Are you sure? I mean, we just met, and what if you don't..."

She cuts me off before I can finish. "Move. In!" she insists.

"Come on," she commands, tossing the paper towel she used to dry her hands into the trash. "Let's go rescue your stuff from that god-awful room."

"But what if...," I stammer, worried her plan might fail before it has a chance to take flight.

"We'll deal with it," she assures me, and my heart swells with so much hope, I might start to cry again. For another person to do something so selfless, to help someone they barely know out of a bad situation, and to be on the receiving end of a kindness of this magnitude... *Is this real?* My high school friends were more of acquaintances than anything else – between my part-time job and school, I didn't have time. It occurs to me I may have never experienced true friendship before.

Gabi looks at me like I imagine an older sister would look at her younger sibling – determined to right this wrong because how dare anyone fuck with her family. *Jesus, it's...*

It's beyond words.

"What do you think?" she presses. "I promise you, I'm normal. Well, I'm sure I have my quirks, but comparatively..."

"Yes," I blurt, cutting her off before she has the chance to change her mind. "If it's okay with you, I'd love to move in."

"Done," she affirms with a self-assured nod. I want to hug her. I want to sob. Her warmth feels like a cradle around my desperate and lonely heart.

"And if anyone tries to move in before your switch is official," she continues, "we'll send them to your old room. You *cannot* stay in that room, Monroe. You'll die of misery before the University processes your switch application. Fuck Dornell for doing this to you and fuck her. Now, let's go get your stuff and get you out of there."

4
KIEREN

"Do you think the Brothers will be mad we didn't come early to help set up?" Jace asks as we stalk through the halls of Monroe's alleged dorm building. She better not have lied to me, but even if she did, I'll find her eventually.

Aww, sweet Jace, always concerned with others' opinions, scared they'll turn against him, just like his father did. Ever the righteous pretty boy with repressed anger issues. It's hard being the unwanted younger brother to the infamous Reid Carver. I'm sure his parents didn't think getting pregnant again six years later was possible, but then, *oopsie*, out came Jace.

"Sigma's waited eighteen years for me to grace them with my presence. They can wait another few hours," I respond flatly. He scoffs a laugh; now used to my humor after four years together in boarding school.

"Who is this girl again?" Jace asks, trailing me.

"Just a friend. Keep up, Jacey," I say over my shoulder.

"Right," he challenges sarcastically. "And would Tierney approve of this *friend*?"

"Who I choose to befriend is of no concern to her," I say dismissively. Admittedly, it was a failure on my part not to end things with Tierney before college, but it's nice to have options, I suppose.

Finally, we're close. Three-twenty-two, Three-twenty-four.... Three-twenty-six.

I knock. Intense music blares from within. Seconds pass, and I knock again, louder this time, in case she didn't hear it over the music. Honestly, I did not peg Monroe for this type of...

The door flies open, and I am blasted with an onslaught of satanic screams atop heavy metal. My ears are so overwhelmed that I don't notice the ghoulish creature standing before me.

"What?" it snarls, and I mean *snarls* in a way I've never experienced. *You don't snarl at me, you goddamn troll.*

I scowl down at the unpleasant face of a girl who is definitely *not* Monroe. Did she lie to me about her room number after all? Perhaps she's cleverer than I initially perceived. She is a CS major, I remind myself.

"I'm looking for Monroe," I practically shout. The door slams in my face.

What in the actual...

I bang on the door until it swings open.

"She's gone," the girl spits. She tries to slam the door shut again, but I'm ready this time.

"Move your foot!" she shouts.

"Listen, Satan's bride," I bark, "just tell me where she is and I'll leave you the fuck alone."

She glares at me, nostrils flaring, but I don't move.

"She moved," she grits.

"Where?" I ask.

"Down the hall with some other girl."

"Again, *where*?" I press. I'd rather not venture any closer to this thing, but if I have to physically get in her face to get answers, I will.

"I don't fucking know and if you don't move your foot, I'll call campus security."

"Campus security?" I mock with laughter. "You think I find the thought of campus security threatening? Who the fuck do you think *he* is?" I ask, jerking my head in Jace's direction. Sweet Jacey makes my menacing ass look like a delight. I'm six-one, and though I haven't measured, Mr. '*Captain of the Andover field hockey team*' has to be at least six-three.

"I'll ask you one more time before I serve your ass a noise citation, where the fuck is Monroe?" I grind out, infuriated by this gatekeeping goblin. My foot remains wedged between her door, and if she doesn't relinquish Monroe's whereabouts in the next five seconds, I'll throw whatever stereo equipment she's got in there out the window and make sure she never makes another peep.

"Down the hall!" the girl exclaims like she's exasperated, but I can see the fear in her eyes at the thought of being reprimanded by the promise of a noise citation. *Or worse.* It's a bold-faced lie because never would I work such a remedial job, but people will believe anything you tell them if you say it with the right amount of conviction.

"I don't know the room number, but it's the one at the very end," she explains in hurried annoyance, like she can't get rid of me fast enough.

Satisfied, I remove my foot, and this unfortunate waste of my time slams the door closed.

I roll my neck and stalk toward the opposite end of the long hallway. A song I recognize grows louder as I approach, followed by the sound of two female voices and the smell of weed.

I knock loudly, and the voices on the other side of the door panic. Hushed curses and scuffled footsteps drown out the music, which has notably been turned down. Their pitiful cover-up attempt is amateur but chucklesome. What if I actually were a Resident Advisor? Their asses would be toast.

The door opens slowly, and perhaps one of the most beautiful women I've ever laid eyes on answers.

"Can I help you?" she asks. Her voice is timid and demure, yet I can tell she's barely able to contain the giggle that wants to burst from her lips. I inhale the scent of freshly sprayed floral perfume laced with notes of marijuana and give her a knowing grin.

"I'm looking for Monroe," I say, keeping my tone steady but firm.

The girl blinks in surprise, then turns to look over her shoulder just as a blonde head peeks out from the side of the room.

She takes one look at me and scrunches her brow. "Kieren?" she asks, confused to see me, I'm sure. But she doesn't know me yet. I've already tracked you down once, Monroe. Is it really such a surprise I would do it again?

I cock my head at her, grinning like a fox that has cornered its prey. "Bad time?" I tease.

I look back at the dark-haired girl who answered the door. "Your room reeks of weed, by the way, so I suggest you let us in, unless you want the smell of pot to fill the entire hallway."

Alarm flickers across her face, and she steps back to let Jace and me through. Monroe straightens herself to sit upright on the bed while the other girl shuts the door behind us.

"What are you doing here?" Monroe asks. Her face remains

scrunched in a scowl as I cross the double room to sit next to her on the bed.

"Are these friends of yours?" the other girls asks Monroe with trepidation. *Little late for that question, don't you think?* I want to say but bite my tongue as I take a seat next to Monroe. She bristles as the mattress dips under my uninvited weight.

"Hardly. I mean,..."

"Hardly?" I scoff at Monroe, leaning back against the wall. "First of all, Monroe, where are your manners? Hi, I'm Kieren," I say to the other girl, waving my hand in greeting. "And this is my friend Jace," I motion. Jace hovers at the edge of the closed door, arms half-crossed like he's not sure what to do with his hands. And dear God, is he fucking blushing?

"Gabriella," the girl says with a wary look. "But you can call me Gabi."

I watch as her sparkling brown eyes turn back to Jace. Inwardly, I shake my head because I know this look. I've seen it for the last four years. Another innocent victim primed for the devastation that is Jace Carver. But why is he just standing there like a clueless dimwit?

"Are you two roommates?" I ask, breaking the awkward tension. Monroe remains stiff as a board beside me, and Jace, who usually never misses an opportunity to flaunt his God-given talents, has gone mute.

"Unofficially," Gabi answers as she strides toward the bed opposite Monroe and plops down. "Come in, make yourselves comfortable."

I'm perfectly comfortable where I am, so I assume this comment is directed at the frozen statue idling awkwardly by the door.

Jace manages the wherewithal to snap out of his trance and approaches Gabi. "Can I sit here?" he asks, motioning to the unoccupied end of her bed.

"Yeah, of course," she smiles, scooting down to make room. He lowers himself with care, politely sitting on the edge of the mattress, and the way Gabi's face flushes at his near proximity makes my lips curl upward.

"How do you know each other?" Gabi asks again, but I'm too focused on Jace's comical nervousness to deign a response.

"Hold on, can we go back to the unofficial roommates comment?" I ask instead, smirking at what might be a once-in-a-lifetime occurrence.

My gaze flicks to Monroe's profile. "Is this not your actual room?"

"I'm going to apply for a room switch once classes start," Monroe answers, refusing to fully face me.

"And until that can happen and it's officially approved," Gabi chimes, "we're unofficial."

"You mean you still technically live down the hall with that troll?"

Gabi bursts out laughing, but Monroe is pensive.

"Technically, yes," she answers, picking at a piece of loose thread on the bedspread.

So, she didn't lie to me. Interesting. Perhaps not clever then. Or maybe she wanted to be found after all.

"Were you looking for me?" Monroe asks, her brow furrowed as she continues her plight, clearly determined to set the thread free.

"Obviously," I answer.

"Why?" she scoffs, like my desire to see her is ridiculous.

"Because I gave you my number, but you never texted," I respond.

"Wow, so you thought you'd track me down? You know, when a girl doesn't text you, typically that's called a rejection," she grins, and although she's still preoccupied with that goddamn thread, I can sense my tenacity has worked its charm.

"Ouch!" Jace bellows from across the room. I see my wingman has finally remembered that he can fucking speak. "That's a term Kieren's never heard before!"

I give him a mocking sneer. Glad to see your balls have returned at my expense, Jacey.

I study Monroe's side profile and sensing my stare, she turns her head to face me. Dark blue eyes find mine – the kind of blue that reminds me of the ocean before a storm. Brooding and secretive, roiling with a thousand unsaid words, churning with unleashed mayhem.

And *fuck. Those fucking lips.*

Goddamn this woman. I can barely contain myself, failing miserably at my usual banter.

"Are you rejecting me, Monroe?" I swallow, steering my dissolute mind back on course. I know she's not turning me away, but I want to hear her admit it out loud. "Because Jace and I can leave if you want."

Her expression softens, and the corners of her mouth twitch upward. "We were getting ready to leave, actually."

"Oh yeah? To where?" I probe.

"A party," she says as she bats her lashes like a coy little minx.

"Funny, because Jace and I wanted to invite you to *our* party."

"Where is *your* party?" Gabi asks. I'm not sure I appreciate this girl's haughty tone.

"Sigma," I respond flatly.

Gabi looks at me, wide-eyed. "Sigma?" she asks with disbelief. "You can get in there?"

Jace snorts a laugh.

"What's so funny?" Monroe cuts in, unamused. Her nose

crinkles when she furrows her brows, and I wonder if she knows how goddamn cute she looks, *like a fucking snack.*

Jace is seconds away from launching into an unnecessary response when I cut him off.

"It's clear you're not interested," I say abruptly, and make a show of scooting to the edge of the bed like I'm seconds away from standing to leave. "Come on, Jace, let's go."

"Are you serious?" Monroe asks with an attitude I fondly remember from the Sigma return to campus barbecue.

"Where else were you planning to go? Let me guess, DKE?" I joke, because I know that asswipe of a frat is having a party tonight.

The two girls exchange an uneasy glance.

"Oh God," I bemoan. "Really? That place?"

Neither girl moves, unclear as to why they've made a poor decision.

"You don't want to go to DKE," Jace offers quietly to Gabi with a shake of his head.

"Why?" she half-whispers.

"Enough chit-chat, do you want to come with us or not?" I say, playing into my aggravation.

"Well, we still have to get dressed," Gabi says hesitantly.

"How long will that take?" I ask.

"Ten minutes," she responds. It's more of a question than answer as Gabi looks to Monroe for confirmation.

"Okay, so get dressed," I order, not giving them the chance to back out. "We'll wait in the hall."

I turn to face Monroe, who glares at me, rightfully so. My behavior is gruff, but we need to get this show on the road. On the other side of the room, I hear Gabi and Jace whispering to each other, so I seize this opportunity to make a lasting impression.

"Monroe," I say softly so only she can hear. "Don't pretend you aren't happy to see me."

Her glare morphs into a mocking grimace, and I chuckle, leaning in to whisper in her ear, "Wear something cute for me." The searing vitriol on her face at this comment draws an ear-to-ear smile, one I couldn't suppress even if I tried.

"Come on, Jace," I beckon, sauntering to the door. Jace reluctantly follows suit, and I'm sure if he had it his way, he wouldn't leave Gabi's bed.

"Ten minutes," I remind them as I open the door. I give Monroe one last over-the-shoulder glance and toss that beautiful, seething face of hers a devilish wink.

5
KIEREN

Monroe holds my hand as I lead her through the back door of a packed Sigma. The progress we made between the beginning of the night and now is remarkable, but I made sure to be on my best, most chivalrous behavior during the drive over to counterbalance my earlier churlishness.

Jace and Gabi follow not far behind. I predict Gabi climbs Jace like a tree before the end of the night, which is typically how nights go for him. Pussy has always come easily for Jace – not that it doesn't come easily for me. I just happen to be more selective. But my boy Jace looked more smitten than usual back in their dorm room. I wonder if he might finally catch feelings for a girl and decide she's worth more than twenty-four hours of his time.

I glance back to see Monroe taking in the surroundings with a look of intrigue mixed with apprehension. I can't say I blame her. Most find Sigma intimidating, and the last time she was here, it was in the middle of the day. Some are awestruck by its majesty – part Gothic castle, part underground cult. It's a sight to behold, really, even in its current tame version. Just wait until I sink my teeth into this place as fraternity president. I grin as the word *'foreboding'* comes to mind.

Club music and strobe lights pulse as I lead us toward the bar area, where sophomore brothers pose as bartenders. Underclass brothers usually suffer through a year of brutal servitude to the fraternity until the next pledge class arrives. The worst stint happens right after joining Sigma during the second semester of one's freshman year, when you become a subservient bitch to the already scorned, humiliated, and degraded pledge class above you. Hell hath no fury like a second-semester sophomore in Sigma, and something tells me this year will be particularly nightmarish with Knox Sterling behind the wheel as president.

I don't know Knox well, not yet anyway, but everyone in the upper echelon of society is familiar with the Sterling family – descendants of Scottish royalty who wield considerable political power both stateside and across the pond. Having run into him at a few parties in Manhattan over the years, he comes across as a cavalier prick, which I can't imagine will bode well for someone like me during the pledge process, who is equally, if not more, supercilious.

Speaking of Knox, I have yet to spot his arrogant ass, which I assume means the upperclassmen are still upstairs, waiting for the perfect time of night to descend upon the drunken and defenseless herd like wolves.

"Don't accept drinks from anyone but me," I shout against Monroe's earlobe as I hand her a vodka soda and pass the other two drinks to Jace and Gabi. She looks up at me while she sips from the thin black cocktail straw.

"Should we take shots?" Gabi asks with a broad smile. Unlike Monroe, who doesn't seem to know much about the Greek scene at Dornell, Gabi was beside herself with excitement when Jace confessed he and I are both Sigma legacies – double legacies to be exact.

I answer Gabi with a "no," but Jace has already ordered shots for the four of us. Whatever. One shot won't impair me too much.

I've mostly stopped using recreational substances since I crashed my car into a telephone pole last year. Fortunately, by some grace of God that I didn't deserve, I wasn't recklessly speeding. If I had been, I likely would have killed both Tierney and myself. I walked away with two broken ribs and a broken jaw. The ribs healed, but my jaw alignment never returned to what it was before the accident. Now I'm left with chronic TMJ pain, but I pop ibuprofen like candy, so I manage just fine. At least, that's what I tell myself.

Speaking of Tierney, that nightmare in waiting is around here somewhere. I scan the dance floor, now a thrashing mass of bodies.

"Monroe, let's go dance!" Gabi begs, grabbing Monroe's hand. She throws me a questioning glance over her shoulder, then follows Gabi into the crowd, and I can't help but swell with triumph. That's right, Monroe. I'm the one you look to now for approval.

Jace crosses his arms as they disappear. "What are the odds they come home with us tonight?" he asks.

"For you? I'd say pretty good," I respond. "I'm not so sure about me."

"I'd say your odds are dece... never mind," Jace says, quick to correct himself. We both simultaneously clock an approaching Tierney flanked by two girls I've never seen before.

"Tierney," I say, addressing her with a false smile I'm sure she notices. I make no effort to disrupt my casual lean against the bar as I remain laser-focused on Monroe's flushed face, worried to lose sight of her in the crowd. "I see you've found new minions."

"Who's the girl?" she glowers.

"Who?" I feign confusion with a tilt of my head.

She gives me a sinister grin. "The Goldilocks one standing here five seconds ago."

"Oh, that one," I say. "She's cute, right?"

Tierney scowls. "Fuck you, Kieren."

"Sorry, T. I think our days of fucking are over."

"I'd throw this drink at you," she grits, "but you're not even worth wasting whatever bottom-shelf swill they're serving here. This frat is a joke."

"Hey," Jace snaps. "Watch your fucking tone, Tierney."

"Fuck you, Jace," she spits.

"Not in a million years," he retorts.

Tierney whirls and stomps away. The two other girls trail her around the edge of the dance floor and out of sight. I have no ill will toward Tierney, but I can't say I feel anything positive for her either. We've had our fun, but now my interests reside elsewhere.

"We should find them," I say to Jace, pushing off the bar when I realize I did indeed lose sight of Monroe. I force my way through thrashing bodies until we're standing in the middle of the dance floor and Monroe is nowhere to be found.

"Did you get Gabi's number?" I shout.

Jace nods and pulls out his phone. We press our way out toward the stairs. If they were lured away by one of the junior or senior brothers, upstairs would be the first place to look. Jace stops mid-step, texting someone I hope is Gabi.

"They're in Seth's room," Jace says, pocketing his phone.

I should have guessed. The current president of Sigma has a knack for seducing even the most resistant of women. It's too bad he's graduating this year. He was a senior at Andover when Jace and I were freshmen, and also a Sigma legacy – one of the few who had a shot at restoring Sigma to its glory if it weren't for the hazing incident two years ago. Ever since an unsuspecting professor thought to take a shortcut through the woods behind Sigma and found himself attacked by naked pledges posing as guard dogs, the University has restricted Sigma's charter. At least they didn't revoke it this time.

That will end soon, though, when the new Dean of Students begins his post at the end of the calendar year, and Knox takes over as president. As much as Knox gets under my skin with his aristocratic golden-boy act, I hope his reign is a step in the right direction toward restoring Sigma's lethal power. Although, no reign will be as lethal and renowned as mine, of course. Word has it that the new Dean of Students is open to absolving the restriction on Sigma's charter if presented with the right motivation. Money is a powerful motivator, as they say, and I love a man who can be bought.

Seth's suite is packed as we shove our way inside. The president of Sigma has his own common room, which is attached to a generous bedroom. "Kieren!" Seth exclaims as he approaches us. He draws out my name like I'm a long-lost friend. "Missed you tonight during set-up," Seth chides.

"Sorry. Had to handle some pressing personal business," I respond.

"And would that pressing personal business happen to involve those two?" Seth asks, pointing toward the far end of the common room.

I tense at the way he says, "*those two,*" like it's open season and Monroe and Gabi are prime targets.

"Maybe," I say. He gives me a deviant grin as he takes a sip of his drink.

"They said they came here with you and Jace. Are they claimed yet?" he asks.

"Do not," I snarl.

"Up for grabs, then," he smirks.

"Seth," I snap. "No."

"You're the one who brought them here, Kieren. You of all people should know better."

Rage crackles beneath my fingertips because Seth's right. Bringing them here tonight, before Jace and I have staked our claim, was a mistake. I look over to see Jace has already made his way to Gabi and wedged himself in next to her on the couch like he plans to make himself fucking comfortable. Absolutely not.

"We need to get them out of here," I bark as I approach Jace and the two girls, not giving a fuck who hears me.

"They're fine. No one's going to touch them while we're here," Jace says, brushing off the concern.

"You know that's not true. They're unclaimed," I hiss, leaning in closer. Jace gives me a scolding look to keep my mouth shut lest the girls overhear, but Gabi and Monroe learning of our intentions is the least of our concerns right now.

"Kieren!" Gabi exclaims, just now clocking my presence, and *fuck me*. Monroe looks concerningly drunk. "We did more shots!"

"Yeah, I bet you did, Gabi." I shoot Jace a look that says, "*I told you so.*"

"I did… two more shots," Monroe says, swaying slightly.

"Right, by *'we'* I meant Monroe." Gabi bursts into laughter. "She took my shot for me."

I have no idea why this is funny.

"Monroe, we need to go," I say tersely.

"No! I don't want to leave!" Gabi protests.

"I don't give a fuck what you do, Gabi, but your friend here is about ten minutes away from blacking out, and I need to get her home."

"Easy, Kieren," Jace says. "How about I stay with Gabi and you can take Monroe home?"

"I don't have a key," Monroe slurs.

"What?" I belt, trying to comprehend her drunken garbles.

"Room key. Don't have it," she explains, but I'm still fucking confused.

"The whole unofficial roommates thing, remember?" Gabi says. "She doesn't have a key to our room yet."

Right. "That's fine. She can crash with me."

"Nooo...," Monroe says with a dramatic shake of her head, and I can tell her situation is getting worse by the minute.

I look down at her, and though I doubt she's in any condition to make decisions, I ask, "Easy way or hard way, Monroe?"

She peers up at me with the same furrowed brows and crinkled nose from earlier.

"Hard way," she manages to say.

"Alright, that's it then."

Before she can comprehend my movements, I pull her up by her armpits and squat to wrap my arms around her upper thighs, then sling her over my shoulder. It was a massive gamble on my part, but not because of the weight. This little thing hardly weighs as much as a medium-sized dog. Throwing an inebriated girl over one's shoulder is asking to get puked on, and I've partied enough during my high school years to have witnessed the horror of a puke-drenched backside.

"Kieren!" she wails like an insubordinate toddler as I part the crowd.

I get halfway to the stairwell when she starts kicking.

"Monroe, I swear to fuck, if you kick me, you're going home in the fucking trunk."

That quiets her.

We make it down three flights of stairs before I hear the strained and desperate warning of, "I'm going to throw up."

I try to set her down, but she can barely stand.

"Almost to the car, baby. Can you make it?"

She nods, but I know my window shrinks by the second. I pick her up again and carry her in my arms until we reach a fire door that I hope opens to the outside of the house. Pressing the door lever with my back, we stumble into the humid night. I look around, unsure at first where we are, until I realize we exited the side of the house that faces the woods.

The rear parking lot is a solid fifty yards away. Too far. I set Monroe down, and she immediately turns around and vomits. Holding her hair, I rub her back as she heaves, cringing as puke splatters violently on the grass. I have no idea if the other two shots were drugged, which is definitely a possibility if she took them in Seth's room, or if she's just a lightweight. Either way, I'm sure this isn't the night either of us planned.

Monroe's head lolls to the side as I carefully take the next curve. Mascara pools under her eyes, creating an unfortunate raccoon effect. Even at her worst, though, she's still so fucking adorable.

I park behind my dorm and walk around to open the passenger door for her.

"We're home, baby," I coax. She swats my hand away as I try to unbuckle her seatbelt.

"I know it's hard, but trust me. You don't want to sleep in the car overnight. I've done it and I can't say I recommend."

She groans begrudgingly, and I help her swivel her legs around so that they hover above the pavement.

"Ready? I'm going to pull you up," I say.

Gently, I tug her forward. She stumbles into my chest, wrapping her arms around my torso. Although I wish the circumstances were different, I can't say I don't enjoy seeing Monroe like this, helpless and needy.

Slowly, we walk through the parking lot and indoors, and after what feels like eons, make it to my room. The walk must have reinvigorated Monroe, because five minutes ago, drunk Monroe could barely stand. Now, drunk Monroe has morphed into sloppy and flirtatious, undeterred by the fact that I watched her puke forty-five minutes ago.

"Let's get you into a T-shirt," I say as I pull an old Andover shirt from my drawer, knowing I won't mind throwing the shirt away if it falls victim to another round of vomit.

She struggles to pull the strappy tank top she wore tonight over her head.

"Here, I can help you," I offer. The feeling of her warm skin as my fingertips graze the sides of her ribcage sends my heart racing. She lifts her arms as I cajole the form-fitting material up and over her head. In Monroe's defense, and unbeknownst to me, there's a hidden layer of tit restraint built into this thing, like a sports bra, and it does take considerable tugging to wrench it off.

Once I've beaten this tank top into submission, her two teardrop-shaped breasts fall free, and I have to swallow the overwhelming urge to push her backward onto the bed. The ache I feel to wrap my mouth around one of her pert breasts coils in my groin.

In no world can I keep helping her take her clothes off and maintain control of myself, so sleeping in her jean shorts will have to suffice for tonight, although I hate the thought of hard pants co-mingling with the soft bedsheets.

She smiles at me like she knows my secret. "You want me," she taunts, leaning back on her elbows. *Fuck, yes, it's all I want.*

I hold the opening of the T-shirt over the crown of her head and help her hands through the arm holes.

"You're drunk," I reason. "Very drunk."

"Aren't you?" she grins and reclines until her back is flat against the bedspread. The natural weight of her breasts causes them to slide up her chest as she lies down, visible even from underneath the thick cotton. My cock strains in agony at the sight, demanding I unzip my shorts.

"Not in the slightest," I swallow, reining in my desire. "I just drove us home, remember?"

Confusion flickers across her face. No, she doesn't remember, and that's probably for the best. I set her purse on my desk along with a bottle of water and ibuprofen as she gazes glassy-eyed up at the ceiling. Walking back to my dresser, I pull out an extra toothbrush from my stash of toiletries along with a tube of toothpaste and set both by her purse as well.

Her head rests on my pillow now, drifting to one side, and her features have softened to the point of angelic, not the usual disapproving and pissed off look she wears like she's annoyed with the ineptitude of the world. It must be a defense mechanism, a cover-up for her insecurities, perhaps.

I study her face for a few more breaths, watching as her eyelids become too heavy to keep open and at last, her body surrenders. How peaceful she looks. How naive and trusting. The sight of her, the subtle rise and fall of her chest, the innocent part of her lips...

Fuck, this woman. I want to sink my teeth into her. I want to do unspeakable things to her. Wrong things. Carnal things. Things she is most definitely not ready to do.

But I must control myself this time. Be patient.

I honestly have no idea how I'm going to manage either of those endeavors, but fuck, I have to try. Look how pure she is, how perfect.

A searing pain thumps in my chest as I watch her sleep, so visceral that staggering over to Jace's bed is as far as I can convince my body to go.

As I ruminate on my good fortune, at how our paths crossed truly by chance, a second notion begins to creep through the caverns of my consciousness. The more I dwell on it, the more I'm unable to ignore it, and I can't shake the feeling that this woman is both my beginning and my end; that we were meant to meet at that barbecue, that she will become the fire that gives me life.

But she will also become the bullet that brings me death.

6
MONROE

My eyelids flutter open, and dread overtakes my body. *Where am I?*

Searing panic floods my mind, and my skin flushes with heat. I'm too terrified to move. My eyes bounce around the room, desperate to make sense of my surroundings. Details are muted with shadow. The room is dark, save for a few slivers of light draped along the wall opposite where I lie.

Cautiously, I wiggle my arm out from under the pillow beneath my head and slowly prop myself up to a seated position. I'm in a boys' room. I have to be. The faint smell of men's cologne lingers in the air, a jumble of sports equipment rests in the corner, and the sheets covering my legs are a dark blue.

Oh God, how much did I drink last night? What is this T-shirt I'm wearing? This isn't mine.

A noise from the other side of the room startles me. Squinting to see through the dim light, I realize another *person* is sleeping, thankfully on the other side of the room and not in bed with me. *Who is that?* Swirling, black tattoos cover the parts of the person's back not concealed by bedsheets. And, oh my God. *Where is my phone? Where are my things?* Frantically, I scan the floor, and a screaming pain blooms at my temples from the sudden eye movement.

I slowly, quietly, peel the sheet off my legs and swivel them forward to hover above the floor. The soles of my feet press against the cool concrete. I wince as the bed makes a creaking sound when I stand. I reach down to scoop up my tank top when the body across the room stirs. My arms freeze mid-reach, and my heart pounds in my chest. Motionless, I wait for the body to move again.

After several long seconds, I make a second attempt to pick up my top, this time successful, and notice my purse is resting on the desk beside the bed. Tiptoeing over, I see whoever put my purse here also left me a toothbrush, toothpaste, a bottle of ibuprofen, and water. Jesus. Was I *that* bad last night?

I stealthily fist my purse, careful not to make any unnecessary noise. The toothbrush and toothpaste are quiet enough to take, but the bottle of ibuprofen will rattle around if touched, and I can't risk waking the tattooed ogre. I have to get out of here.

My fingers wrap around the doorknob, praying it won't make a loud sound when I twist, but dammit, it clicks. The body stirs again, but this time, instead of waiting, I pull open the door, shut it, and flee.

I scurry down the hall without a semblance of a plan. My bare feet pad against the rough carpet, which is no doubt filthy, but seeing as I'm wearing a man's T-shirt, shorts from last night, and no shoes, I haven't the time to dally on hygiene. It occurs to me that I should look at my phone, but there's no way in hell I'm stopping to do so in the hallway.

Toward the end of the corridor, a restroom placard hangs from the ceiling. I press forward, my scamper now almost a jog, and dart inside. I don't know why I was practically running. It's not like anyone was chasing me, but I couldn't shake the thought of that person in the room waking at the sound of my departure and then stalking after me.

I drop my tank and purse in a pile at my feet, then unscrew the toothpaste cap. I am a mess. I am disgusting. My skin feels sticky with last night's sweat, and now all I can picture is my skin covered in a congealed slime concocted from shame and regret.

More horror unfolds when my eyes flick up to see my reflection in the mirror. The T-shirt says fucking Andover. *Really? Really Monroe?*

Goddammit.

I can't. I can't stay in this T-shirt for a second longer, so in my compromised state, I decide getting in the shower – *the shower* – with no towel, no change of clothes, no soap, *nothing*, is the right idea. In fact, it's the only idea that makes any fucking sense, like an intrusive thought I must see through to completion lest I explode.

Water roars to life. Before stepping under the harsh, scalding spray, I manically press the lever of the hand soap dispenser, convinced a vicious scrubbing will undo whatever terrible decisions were made last night.

Did I hook up with Kieren? *Have sex with him?* That was Kieren, right? Fuck, I honestly don't know.

I scrub harder. When the hand soap I pilfered runs out, because, yes, I decided hand soap was just as good as body wash in this moment, I step out of the shower, naked and not giving a fuck, to hysterically pound the lever of the dispenser for more.

Finally satisfied I've cleansed myself of sin, I turn off the shower and wring out my hair, grateful that if nothing else, this oversized Andover T-shirt can double for a towel.

I don't bother putting my underwear back on and hike the

coarse jean material over my wet legs. The thought of also wrangling with my tight tank top from last night, trying and failing to pull it over my damp skin, is immediately too daunting. My makeshift towel will become my shirt once more, even if it is now unfortunately see-through in the worst of spots. *Of course.*

Whatever, my time to flee is now. I scoop up my belongings and poke my head out of the restroom entrance, scanning in either direction. Which way did I come from initially? Everything looks the same. I'm sure I'll eventually find an exit.

Just as I begin my escape, I hear, "Monroe."

I halt at the sound of my name, wincing at the conviction in his voice, the stern, scolding tone.

Slowly, like a reprimanded child caught stealing candy, I turn around. Kieren, shirtless and bearing a chest full of tattoos, strides toward me with a look of annoyance on his face.

"What the fuck, Monroe? Were you seriously going to Irish goodbye?"

"I...," I stammer, unable to find words.

"Hold on. Did you *shower*?" he asks derisively.

"Umm..." I can't answer, mortified by my own actions.

He scans me head to toe, and I watch in horror as his eyes land on the objects I have haphazardly clutched in my right hand.

"Next time you decide to do a walk of shame, Monroe, you might want to put these in your pocket," he chides, effortlessly plucking my black lace thong free.

My eyes flare wide at my own carelessness. I'm practically waving my underwear like a flag. *Jesus.*

"Come on, let's get you out of the hallway. I can't have you walking around in public in a see-through T-shirt."

Embarrassment wrenches at my throat, and I can hardly

swallow as I look down at my chest, cringing at the transparent patches of fabric over my nipples. Kieren has already begun walking, my underwear fisted in his hand, and, unable to sort through any other viable options, I follow.

Walking back into the room where I awoke feels both strange and familiar. I can't quite sort out what I'm doing here, or why I'm still here, but I also feel like I want to stay. Oddly, I feel a sense of comfort around Kieren, even though I hardly know him, but a part of me wants to curl up next to him, close my eyes, and go back to sleep.

"I set out some pain pills," Kieren says as he sits down on the bed where I slept. "You should take them."

I suppose that would be prudent since my head has yet to stop throbbing, and my hangover seems to worsen by the second.

"How much of last night do you remember?" he smirks, amused by my struggle to twist-off the childproof cap.

"Not much," I admit, finally getting the bottle open.

"Probably for the best," he says, the smile in his voice somehow makes my head pound harder.

"What happened?" I ask, tossing back a few pills and chugging half the bottle of water.

"Do you really want to know?"

"Well, I mean, I know I was a mess, but did we..." I pause nervously.

"Fuck?" he finishes for me.

I nod.

"No, Monroe, and I'm a bit offended you think I'm the type of guy who would take advantage of you in that way. Now, the other guys at the party last night, they would have fucked you without a second thought. Most of them would fuck a corpse if it were in front of them."

I wince, horrified by the visual of a strange man fucking my lifeless body.

"Thank you for helping me," I mutter, ashamed by how reckless I acted.

"Hey, come here," he says, reaching for my hand. I follow his pull as he guides me onto his lap in a straddle, drinking in his defined muscles and tattoos. I did not peg prep-school Kieren as the type of boy who would have tattoos, and certainly not this many.

"Do you normally drink like that?" he asks sincerely, brushing my sopping wet hair away from my face.

"No. Honestly, I really didn't drink in high school."

"So, you're a good girl?" he smirks, searching my eyes.

I look down, avoiding his probing gaze.

"No? You're not?" he jests.

"I'm not sure what you're asking me," I say. I look up to meet his eyes, but can only focus on his dark brown irises for a few seconds before feeling forced to look anywhere else. My pulse quickens at how intimate this conversation feels.

His broad palms skim up my outer thighs, stopping just below my shorts. He caresses my skin, delicately, intentionally, and I feel him start to get hard underneath me. I shift awkwardly, unsure of the proper response in these situations. Is it normal for college kids to have sex without formally dating? And is sex where this is headed?

"Kieren," I say, apprehensive.

"Are you a virgin, Monroe?"

"No, but..."

"But what?"

I squirm, embarrassed by my inexperience. "I've only had sex two times. Well, once, really, unless twice in one night with the same person counts as two times."

"And did you come?" He asks this so casually, I laugh.

"What? I don't know!" I respond, blushing with shame at my lack of knowledge.

"It's a yes or no question, Monroe. You either did or you didn't."

"How would I know?" I stammer.

He furrows his brows at me. "Are you serious?"

I make an exasperated huff. My closest friend for the last six years was my elderly grandmother, who was always home and always around. I was too self-conscious and paranoid to do much exploring on my own. The only reason I had sex was due to desperation, because for some inexplicable reason, I was determined not to start college a virgin.

"Kieren!" I squeal as I'm tossed from his lap and onto my back.

Kieren's mouth is pressed against my abdomen a second later, kissing my skin as he lifts the damp T-shirt up over my breasts. He shifts upward, hovering over my chest as he circles my breast with two tender kisses and then wraps his full mouth around my nipple. My back bows as he sucks, writhing as his firm hand simultaneously squeezes my other breast.

"Is this okay, Monroe?" he asks, his mouth finding mine as he continues to play with my left nipple.

Heat flushes my skin as my nipples harden in response to his touch.

"Kieren," I stammer, pulling away. "I don't...,"

"I'm not ready for sex yet," I say, swallowing my nerves, worried what I said will upset him.

"That's okay," he says gently as he kisses my jawbone. "We'll wait."

Relief floods my body. Thank God. He's not angry; he understands.

"Can I take these off?" he asks, skimming his fingers down my stomach until they land at the top button of my shorts.

"Okay," I breathe.

His unflinching eyes search mine. "Are you sure?"

I nod, although I don't feel fully confident in my response.

"We'll take this slow," he reassures me, unzipping my shorts and pulling them down over my legs. "Tell me to stop at any time, and I will."

"Oh my God, Monroe," Kieren groans with admiration as he studies my half-naked form. His words sound like praise, and my body swells with warmth in response.

He shifts forward, his torso pressed against mine. "So beautiful," he whispers, kissing me with a need I feel deep within my bones. I've never been kissed like this before, with passion and heat and a desire that feels smoldering.

I gasp against his mouth at the feeling of fingers sliding between my labia.

"Kieren," I breathe, wrapping my arms tighter around his shoulders as his fingers dip slightly inside my entrance.

"Shhh, it's okay. I only want to lubricate my fingers with your arousal," he explains in such a matter-of-fact way that I'm instantly soothed.

"Does this feel good?" he asks as he swirls those same fingers methodically atop my clit.

"Yes," I admit.

"Relax, Monroe," he coaxes as he kisses the area where my jaw meets my neck. "It doesn't happen in thirty seconds, unless you're using a vibrator or wand, which I have, but just not here."

I nod, feeling painfully self-aware.

"May I use my mouth?" he whispers.

"Okay," I agree. It's so polite, so considerate...

My breath hitches as his warm breath tickles my skin, and then *my God...*

I can't stop the moan that rumbles up my throat when his

tongue, wet and hot, envelops my clit. I fist the sheets under my palms as he licks and sucks at pace that is perfectly steady. Having a man, or anyone for that matter, eat my pussy is also something I've yet to experience, and goddamn, how can something feel this good? My body begins to react to the continuous pressure and stimulation in a way that's hard to describe.

As if sensing this, Kieren dips the same two fingers barely inside my entrance, stimulating the rim of my vagina with delicate, curling strokes. Prickling heat radiates outward, up toward my belly button, down the tops of my thighs, and then inside my core in a building spasm. My breath has become choppy, and a gasp escapes my lips as the spasm at my base becomes overwhelming. My entire center is quivering when...

High-pitched, breathy moans spill from my lips at the pulsing sensation that overtakes my pussy – it's like I have an animal between my legs with a mind of its own. My pussy clenches and pulses, and I am certain, *positive*, that I have never felt anything this euphoric before in my life. I strain for breath, thinking the sensation is subsiding, when I'm rocked again, quivering like an earthquake aftershock.

The world momentarily stops, leaving me dizzy but effervescent, and I'm faintly aware of my heaving chest as I close my eyes, savoring this feeling.

Kieren dips his fingers inside me, and I whimper.

"Open your eyes, Monroe," he says, his gaze now level with mine.

He holds two fingers up for me to see, both visibly coated with a sheen.

"This is what your cum looks like," he says, pausing to make sure I acknowledge the slightly milky substance on his fingers.

"This is what it feels like," he says, swiping his index finger over my lower lip. The viscous slickness of my orgasm is apparent even without pressing my lips together.

"And this is what you taste like," he says, parting my lips. My eyes flutter closed as I press my tongue against that same index finger and suck. Are all college boys this sensual? This can't be the norm.

I open my eyes as he pulls his finger from my mouth and watch him bring his still-coated middle finger to his lips. The expression on his face as he sucks his finger clean leaves me breathless.

"Do you know what I think you taste like, Monroe?" Kieren asks, pulling me out of daze.

I shake my head, mesmerized by the glowing intensity of his eyes.

He grins as he lowers his chest. His lips graze my ear, and my breath catches in anticipation.

"You taste like mine."

7
KIEREN

The problem with inexperience is that it's both a blessing and a curse – a blessing because she's trainable. I can mold her to like the things that I like. A curse because we have to ease into the hard stuff.

I can't strap a ball gag around her mouth and choke her while her pussy strangles my cock anytime soon, but the prospect of turning such an innocent little thing into a deviant like me is worth the wait. To not have even experienced the most basic of orgasms at her age is both astonishing and a tragedy.

On top of that, she's undeniably gorgeous, and I cannot fathom how this lack of experience happened. I mean, her body is fucking flawless, and I intend to own every inch of it, but how did she not have guys lined up outside her door at the ready?

I look down at her as we walk back to her dorm, and she smiles up at me. I return her smile, grinning at the possibility of what we could become. How perfect we will look together.

Our future unfolds in my mind's eye as we walk, on our

way to rescue Jace from whatever chokehold Gabi's pussy has over him. *I have such big plans for you, my pretty little Monroe.*

"Can I ask you something?" she asks out of the blue.

"Okay," I respond hesitantly.

"How did you get so many tattoos? You definitely started getting them before you became an adult, right? Did one of your parents go with you?"

"Absolutely not." I laugh at the absurd thought of my mom coming with me to get tattooed. She would faint.

"Then how?"

"The same way I can buy alcohol or cigarettes if I want."

"So, you have a fake I.D.?"

"Don't you?"

"No," she admits.

"Hmm, that's a problem," I ponder out loud.

"And your parents never saw your tattoos?"

"I'm sure they caught glimpses of them, but it's my grandfather who thinks tattoos are a disgrace. That's why I only have tattoos on my chest and back. And as long as I'm not pissing off my grandfather, my dad doesn't give a shit."

"Did they hurt?"

"Some more than others, but after the first thirty minutes, adrenaline kicks in and you start to numb out. I kind of like it, though – the pain of needles entering my skin. It's calming. I think that's why I have so many. Is that weird to say?"

I look down at her contemplative expression.

"I get it," she says, but I can tell she's chewing on my admission, perhaps wondering if she should find it disturbing.

"You get it because you also like the feeling of pain?" I ask to ward off any concerning thoughts that might be percolating in her brain.

"What?" she asks on a choked laugh, looking up at me.

"You said so at the barbecue when we first met. I asked you

why you chose to be a CS major, and you said it was because you like pain."

"Oh," she says, scrunching her face. "I don't know why I said that. I think I was trying to make a joke."

We walk several steps in uncomfortable silence. "Or maybe it's because...," She lingers on her last word, debating if she should say more.

"Because?" I probe.

"Nothing," she dismisses, her eyes focused on the floor ahead, determined not to look at me.

"Monroe," I say sternly, fixated on her blank expression.

"Monroe," I press again, studying her face for any sign of awareness, but her mind is preoccupied elsewhere.

Finally, I snap a finger in front of her face. She shoots me an annoyed look, but at least she's returned from zombie land or wherever her head went.

"Another time, Kieren," she chastises, her tone curt and silencing. It surprises me, but I acquiesce. We've made it back to her unofficial room and now is not the time. Still, knowing that this secret, this underlying reason behind her propensity toward pain, lingers between us feels unbearable.

She knocks on her door and follows it with, "Gabi, it's me. And Kieren."

Seconds later, Jace opens the door just wide enough for his body to slip through and quickly pulls it closed.

"Hey Monroe," he says cheerfully. "How are you feeling this morning?"

"Bad," she retorts.

Jace laughs and walks down the hall a few paces to give us space.

"Hey, not bad," I tsk, tilting her chin up with the same two fingers I had buried in her pussy less than an hour ago. God, she was so fucking wet. I couldn't let her go back to her dorm without a round two. The nerves and uneasiness she felt seemed to dissolve entirely after her first release. Her body clearly wanted more, and when she rode my fingers like a needy little slut, it took all my restraint not to whip my dick out and fuck her. But I'm a man of my word. Well, sometimes. Actually, never. *However,* I did promise her we would wait until she was ready, and her perfect fucking pussy is worth the wait. *Goddamn, is it ever.*

"Better," I correct, after sealing our time together this morning with a final kiss.

"Fine, better," she admits, allowing her lips to linger against mine.

"I'll call you later," I say before she slips behind the door and out of sight. One of them, probably Gabi, squeals when the door clicks shut, and I take that as my cue to leave.

"Successful night?" I ask Jace as I catch up to him.

He smirks, looking down at his feet.

"What?" I ask. "Was it not?" Jace usually isn't the gossiping type, but he'll let choice details slip.

"It was good," he says with a sheepish grin.

"Did you fuck her?" I ask bluntly.

He shakes his head, and I'm taken aback.

"Seriously?" I question. "Well, that's a first."

"I swear to God, Kieren, I'm going to marry that girl."

This statement has me confounded. Never has Jace Carver uttered words even remotely in the realm of commitment.

"Are you feeling okay?" I probe. "Feverish, maybe?"

The fucker can't stop smiling. "I'm serious, Kieren. Something about her is... different. I don't know. She does something to me."

I sigh. There goes my best friend. Things with Monroe better fucking work out.

"You two?" Jace inquires with a raise of his brows.

"Oh. Us? Well, Monroe and I aren't quite at the wedding invitation phase yet, but we're making progress."

"She's not your normal type," Jace comments.

"Meaning?"

"Meaning she's not some blood-thirsty, elitist snob who only cares about money and power."

I bristle at his unsolicited judgment. "Let me remind you, Jacey, that you also fall into the category of elitist snob."

"Yeah, because of my parents. But money and power aren't things I personally care about."

"Aww. How idealistic of you," I sneer. "My father didn't give me a choice."

8
MONROE

"I can't wear this," I huff in exasperation, examining myself in the mirror that hangs on the outside of my closet door.

"Are you crazy?" Gabi rebuffs, struggling to find the zipper on the back of her dress.

"Let me help you," I offer.

"Do you think tonight will be the night?" she asks me as I zip her up.

"Maybe," I say. "Kieren's certainly been dropping hints."

"Are you nervous?" she asks.

"Were you nervous with Jace?"

"Yeah, a lot actually," she admits. "I've only had one boyfriend before, in high school, and well...," she trails off. Her eyes grow distant as they find the ground. Gabi's never mentioned this high school boyfriend before, or any past romantic interests for that matter, but the way her brown eyes have glazed over with sorrow makes me think this is an old wound best left alone.

"It's okay, I understand," I say in solidarity. "I told you

about my singular experience this past summer, and it was pretty terrible. It felt so transactional and awkward."

"Did you use protection?" Gabi asks, her voice quiet and concerned.

"Of course, but I also have an IUD. When I turned eighteen, I went to the clinic to get one. Definitely wasn't taking my grandmother with me, which I guess is why I waited so long to, you know...," I explain.

Gabi nods solemnly. "I have one too," she adds. I can tell this is an uncomfortable subject, so I don't pry but also don't know how to react, so I linger by her side with unease.

"Anyway," she states. Her proclamation is abruptly cheerful. "You look unreal in that dress. Seriously, like a goddess. I bet Kieren will throw you over his shoulder the moment he sees you."

I scoff at the thought of Kieren being overcome with need from just the sight of me. It's been a month and a week since Kieren Hunt came into my life, and I still don't know what to make of our relationship. I see how Jace is with Gabi – sweet and kind yet protective. It's clear he's fallen for her, and frankly, I wouldn't be surprised if he professes his love in the next thirty days.

The way Kieren looks at me is different, and I can't put my finger on the feeling. Sometimes I catch him looking at me like he wants to sink his teeth into my neck. Sometimes I'm not sure he's looking at me at all, versus looking right through me. When I catch a glimpse of his glazed-over, indifferent expression, it's crushing. Is he bored with me? I've tried to make myself as compatible as possible for someone like him.

I want him to like me, but part of me feels like I'm performing for Kieren – cosplaying a version of myself to fit the type of girlfriend I think he wants. My hair is always styled, my makeup is always done – even for my seven a.m. class – and, even though I know it's wrong, I've consciously been restricting what I eat. Outwardly, I fit the part, but inwardly, I'm one scathing self-judgment away from crumbling. My hyper sense of self-awareness is exhausting.

I can tell Kieren's frustrated that I haven't given him all of myself yet. It's not for lack of desire. It's because I'm terrified that once I give him this final piece of me, he'll lose interest. I can't explain why I think this, and maybe he won't, but our interactions over the last month have begun to feel strained in a way that makes me feel like he's pulling away. The mere thought of losing him makes me sick to my stomach, which is absurdly frustrating because it shouldn't matter. There are so many other people to meet, my college experience has just begun, yet why is it I lie awake at night, terrified I'll get a text from him telling me it's over?

I look at myself in the mirror while Gabi, standing three feet behind me, does the same.

My dark brown roots are painfully visible, but the worry of finding a local hair stylist within my budget has made me too anxious to search around. Gabi wants me to come home with her next weekend for a self-care trip to wax every unwanted hair from our bodies. It seems like an unnecessary expense when shaving and plucking are practically free. I don't know how to tell her I can't afford any of this, let alone go to a hairdresser in Philadelphia, where her family lives.

My mom was fucking right. I should have kept my brown hair, but I love how the blonde looks on me. It's my favorite personal quality by a landslide, and if I have to forgo other expenses to keep it, like investing in a new pair of sneakers because my current ones are starting to fall apart, I will.

Thankfully, the rest of my dyed-blonde hair, curled into bohemian waves tonight, distracts from my lack of upkeep. I stare at my reflection in a way that feels unsteady. The face looking back at me in the mirror is unrecognizable – cheek contour, overlined lips, and heavy black winged eyeliner. I look painted, and eerily like a doll.

The satin black dress Gabi insisted I wear hugs my body, squeezing my cleavage upward to make room for my lungs and tapering to a tight opening at the knee. I'm also painfully aware that the cost of this dress could cover my next ten hair appointments. When I saw the designer's name on the inside label, I forgot how to swallow. I didn't realize it was normal for eighteen-year-olds to own clothing from Dolce & Gabbana.

Sensing my apprehension, Gabi asks, "Monroe, are you okay? You look so nervous! Do you want to take a shot before the boys get here?"

I nod. I desperately need my anxiety to calm the fuck down.

Maybe it's because my grandmother sounds increasingly disoriented each time I call her. Maybe it's because I feel way over my head in all my classes. Maybe it's Kieren. The thought of him throwing me over his shoulder like a concubine feels like less and less of a possibility with each passing minute. Does he even want me anymore?

I sense myself beginning to spiral, and right on cue, Gabi hands me a shot of vodka, both of us gagging after we throw them back.

"The boys are downstairs," she coughs, looking at her phone. My nerves flutter. I've never been to a formal event like this before. I didn't even go to my prom. I have no idea what I'm supposed to do or how I'm supposed to act.

"Don't worry," Gabi assures me with a final swipe of lip gloss and spritz of floral perfume. "It's all going to be fine."

9
KIEREN

Jace is on edge, and I can't blame him. I don't think either of us expected Reid Carver to make an appearance at Homecoming this year, certainly not this soon post-divorce.

"You look good, Jacey," I offer, patting him on the shoulder as he straightens his tie in the mirror.

"Reid's going to be a fucking nightmare," he grumbles. "I already saw him once today when we were setting up for the alumni mixer, and that was enough. He was already tipsy at ten a.m., so he must be out of his mind by now."

"Probably," I agree. "Just keep him away from Gabi. And Monroe, for that matter. Especially Monroe."

"You need to lock that down," Jace says, turning to take his suit jacket off the hanger where it rests.

"You don't need to remind me," I grit. The fact that Monroe has yet to let me fuck her grates against my ego every fucking day. But I made her a promise. An idiotic promise that I regret every goddamn minute because I didn't think she would make me wait this fucking long.

"Beer?" Jace asks, bending down to open the mini fridge.

"No. Driving, remember?"

Jace cracks the can open. "Not even one?"

"Not tonight. Monroe doesn't know this yet, but I'm taking her to Connecticut when we leave the mixer."

Jace chokes on his sip, quickly bending forward to avoid splashing his white dress shirt.

"Why?" Jace coughs. "Are you introducing her to your parents?"

"Fuck no! Could you imagine my dad learning that my girlfriend is not only a poor nobody but a poor nobody with an incarcerated parent?"

"You're a fucking asshole, you know that, Kieren?"

"I do. But most would say that's part of my charm," I quip.

"If not to meet your parents, then why the trip?"

"You know why," I say, popping up the collar of my dress shirt before draping the tie around my neck.

"What, exactly, do you have planned for that girl?"

"A lot," I respond, pulling the ends of the silk tie into position.

"Kieren," Jace says firmly.

I eye Jace in the mirror, holding his stare. Thanks to Tierney's big fucking mouth in high school, he knows the type of bedroom play I enjoy, but I don't appreciate the judgment of my proclivities. I should never have dated her and just stuck to my rotating pool of Manhattan socialites, many of whom were equally as sadistic. Kids raised in New York City grow up differently, it seems, and God bless their little depraved hearts.

"What Jace?" I spit.

"Take it easy with Monroe, okay?"

"Why?" I bark, whirling around. "Are you afraid that I'll scare her off, and Gabi will follow suit? Because maybe you should focus on your own fucking relationship and leave mine alone."

He holds up his free hand in supplication. "Easy," he says. "Gabi and I are solid. I'm just saying, maybe don't bring out the chains on the first night. Where the fuck do you buy those things, anyway? Home Depot?"

I give him a displeased look and turn back toward the mirror to finish my tie. Jace can judge me all he wants, but after a month of waiting and planning – hell, the STD testing alone took a week – I don't plan to let her do anything but take it.

"Reid is up with Seth. I'm going to go say hi," I tell Jace as the four of us stand around a tall, round cocktail table. The back lawn of Sigma has been outfitted in the theme of a summer clam bake. Waitstaff weave through the crowd with platters of mini crab cakes, shucked oysters, and a gray, mushy mixture on saltine crackers, which I'm told is smoked trout dip. An actual bartender doles out chilled IPAs and wine in glassware alongside generous pours of top-shelf whiskey.

Alumni, recently graduated and decades out, are gathered around the lawn wearing similar versions of the same khaki suit. Some stand arm-in-arm with their spouses, who all wear floral cocktail dresses and remind me of my mother's country club friends.

"Okay, I'll stay here and keep Gabi and Monroe company," Jace responds.

"No interest in seeing your big bro again, huh?" I poke.

"No," Jace grumbles with a scathing look.

"Jace, you can go hang out with your brother!" Gabi offers. "Monroe and I will be fine. Besides, it's mostly a bunch of old guys." She motions to the clusters of middle-aged men as if she weren't a lamb standing amid a pack of wolves.

"No, it's better if Jace stays here as your chaperone," I say. I trust not a single fucking person around Monroe. "I'm only going to say hello. Twenty minutes, tops. And don't worry, Jacey, I won't tell Reid you're down here avoiding him," I wink.

Turning my back on the three of them, I make my way up to Seth's room. Fall weather has finally made an appearance, although right now, with the sun in its golden hour, the temperature is hot enough to make formal wear uncomfortable. By the time I reach Seth's common room, my balls are drenched in sweat.

Male voices converse over the obvious sound of someone snorting cocaine. Stepping through the doorway, I see Reid hunched over a silver tray that holds multiple fat lines of white powder.

"Gentlemen," I say, announcing myself.

"Kieren!" Seth exclaims, motioning for me to enter. "Get over here! We were just talking about you."

I scan the faces of the four other alumni sitting on worn furniture clustered around the coffee table. Two of them I recognize – Reid and Colin Coates. Colin is a legend and someone I've heard my father mention often. He graduated five years ago, I believe, and now runs one of the most successful hedge funds in the Tri-State Area.

"Really?" I ask, although I'm not surprised, as I make my way to an open seat. But I know the persona I need to play to win over the group, so I humbly add, "I highly doubt I'm interesting enough to be the topic of conversation."

"We were talking about how it's likely you have a Sigma Key," Seth continues.

"What's a Sigma Key?" I know a lot about this fraternity and its lore, but I've never heard of a *Sigma Key*.

I spare a glance at Reid Carver as I sit down. I know divorces can be brutal, but Christ. His sallow complexion and dark under-eye circles could scare a ghost, which is saying a lot for someone who, like Jace, has light brown skin and looks like a fucking Tom Ford model.

Jace said Reid's been spiraling post-separation, though he's managed to maintain his livelihood working at Crosswater Capital in the Bay Area, making more money than God. I'd feel bad for the guy if he weren't so goddamn untouchable as Topher Krauss' prized underling.

Topher Krauss is the founder of Crosswater Capital, a leading private equity and venture capital firm, and another Sigma alumnus whom my father talks about constantly. You'd think the man knew Topher and Reid personally. Allegedly, according to my dad, Crosswater is on track to rival the most prominent and successful private equity firms in San Francisco. As his employee, and certainly for Reid as his supposed chosen disciple, you can't buy that level of reverence. Hopefully, Jace's older brother doesn't fuck it up while he drowns his sorrows in an eight ball. Maybe he just needs the right rebound to snap him out of his depression, but I doubt there is a woman brave enough to accept the challenge. Pity.

"I'm sorry. A Sigma Key?" I ask again, confirming I heard correctly.

"I'm surprised your grandfather or dad never mentioned this to you," Colin Coates comments.

"No, never," I confirm. "Is it like a literal key?"

"No," Colin draws out, like he's chastising me for not knowing better. "Some of the older Sigma fraternity houses have hidden rooms. I'm assuming this house has one, given it was the Founding Chapter. Early members received secret keys to these rooms, called Sigma Keys. It's not a key like you'd expect to see, but rather it's built into the Sigma ring.

Ask your grandfather to demonstrate how his ring works the next time you see him. It's a sight to behold. I'm sure he was waiting for the right time to tell you about Sigma's ancient traditions. The Ritual of Sacrifice has been a guarded secret of the Sigma since the beginning, but it's not exactly the type of thing you talk about at Thanksgiving dinner."

"The *Ritual of Sacrifice*?" I question. Because what in the actual fuck is this, and why, in my eighteen years of life, did my grandfather not so much as mention this to me? Why do I have to find out about this from Colin fucking Coates, who now no doubt thinks I'm a fucking clueless child? Does my father know about this? Of course, he does, because he wears my grandfather's Sigma ring now. He must know. Leave it to dear old Dad to withhold critical information at my expense.

"I've heard of the Sinners tradition," I quickly say to correct myself. My grandfather *has* alluded to an old tradition of Sigma's that is similar to a modern day Little Sisters' program. Women are initiated into The Brotherhood as members, often paired with an older brother who acts as their mentor, but at the end of the day, it's a fancy term for fucking your way into the cool kids' club. You fuck a god, you become a goddess. That sort of thing.

"Not that one," Reid says with a sniff of his nose, leaning back to take a much-needed pause.

"Then enlighten me," I state, trying to conceal my agitation.

"Blood sacrifice," Colin says nonchalantly. My eyebrows flare in response.

"I know," Colin continues, eyeing my reaction. "It's taboo, but there are those who believe in the cycle of blessings. Elder Sigmas are known to worship a fallen god named Moloch, and it's believed that those who offer blood sacrifices to this god will be rewarded in the form of wealth and power. Hence, the Ritual of Sacrifice."

Taboo? I think blood sacrifice is a bit beyond the scope of being termed *taboo.*

"You're speaking in the present tense," I point out to Colin. "You said '*there* are *those.*' You're not implying this tradition is still practiced even today, are you?"

Colin shrugs with a wicked grin, which is both as perplexing as it is telling.

"So, blood sacrifice and a secret room that can only be opened with a Sigma ring that functions as a key," I summarize. "Sounds about right."

I brush off this revelation, but my mind is spinning with curiosity, and I make a mental note to search every inch of Sigma for this alleged hidden room as soon as fucking possible.

"Do you think you have the balls to bring back the Sinners tradition?" Colin asks pointedly.

"Obviously," I deadpan. This earns a chuckle from Reid. "Jace sure as fuck doesn't," he comments.

"Good. Someone needs to restore this fraternity's power on campus. Maybe then, alumni like us will be more forthcoming with our donations," Colin smirks.

Reid chuckles knowingly, and I clock the unsaid exchange between Reid and Seth.

"What?" I ask. "Does this Sigma chapter have money issues? I thought our coffers were solid."

"Alumni have been withholding donations," Seth responds. "And that includes you fuckers," he says with a glance around the table.

"Bring back our traditions and we'll bring back our donations," Colin says. I inwardly sneer at this asshole's arrogance but am careful to keep my expression neutral as it seems I have much to learn. Yet another reason to despise my fucking father.

I hate being kept in the dark, told I'm too unpredictable, too reckless, too immature to be trusted with serious matters.

"Why not Knox?" I question. "I won't take over as fraternity president for two and a half years."

"He's graduating in May. Going to law school at Stanford," Seth explains.

"Knox has more pressing shit on his plate right now than what's happening here," Reid interjects, his tone oddly condescending. My brows knit together in confusion as I give Reid a leveled look. One minute ago, bringing back Sigma's dark traditions seemed paramount, but now Knox has better things to do? And why does Reid know all this? I didn't realize they had any relationship whatsoever, let alone close enough that Reid feels it necessary to defend how Knox spends his time. Odd.

"And where is this hidden sacrifice room again?" I ask, pivoting the conversation. It honestly sounds ridiculous. Blood sacrifice? Really? But I suppose, given Sigma's history, it tracks.

"No idea, but I'm sure if you ask your grandfather, he'll tell you. You should also ask him about his body count while you're at it."

"His body count?" I scoff. "Why would I care about how many women my grandfather's fucked?"

"No, not that kind of body count," Colin grins.

Reid smirks like he knows something, and Colin leans forward. "How else do you think your granddaddy Hunt got so goddamn rich?"

10
MONROE

Gabi tilts backward in the kind of full-body laugh that makes me wonder what this basic, middle-aged man with red, splotchy cheeks could have possibly said to warrant such an exaggerated response. Jace is turned away, engaged in a separate conversation of his own, and I'm doing my best to maintain my forced smile and follow along. Gabi struck a chord with this man the moment she mentioned she's a business major, and he was more than happy to name-drop his work history.

"Enjoying yourself?"

I startle at the unexpected sound of a male's voice. His tall frame is casually sidled up to the cocktail table I had forgotten was at my back. He looks familiar. I've seen this head of dirty blonde hair before at the Sigma parties I've attended with Kieren, but never up close. His grey-blue eyes glance up at me expectantly as he takes a sip of his drink, and I'm so lost in thought about whether his eyes are more grey than blue or blue than grey that I forget his question entirely.

"What?" I ask awkwardly.

The left side of his mouth quirks subtly upward with the beginnings of a smirk as he lowers his glass. "I asked if you were enjoying the event."

"Oh. Sure. I mean, yes. It's nice. This event."

He laughs through his nose, and heat flushes my face. "That bad, huh?"

"No. Not bad," I say, struggling to get myself together. "I just don't know anyone. Other than Gabi and Jace. And Kieren," I add. More heat sizzles up my neck, and I can feel the sweat at my hairline. Stumbling. I am stumbling all over myself under the unrelenting gaze of this unnervingly composed man.

Get it together, Monroe, I coach myself, determined to make another go at normal conversation.

"You're...?" I begin, raising the pitch of my voice as I linger on my question.

"Knox," he states. "Knox Sterling. I'm a junior."

"Oh, right," I remember. "Kieren told me you're the next president of Sigma."

He gives me a closed-mouth, perfunctory smile. "That's correct. I take over at the start of next semester."

He says this in a way that makes me think he's not thrilled to be the next president, which is curious to me because Sigma is all Kieren seems to care about, so I just assumed everyone else in this fraternity felt the same.

"And you're Monroe? Kieren's girlfriend, yes?" he asks, raising his eyebrows.

"Yeah, I guess. I mean, we haven't really labeled our status yet, but umm...," I trail off with a shrug of my shoulder. I know I gravitate toward awkward, but this is downright embarrassing. What is it about this man that has me so flustered?

Knox is not the type of guy I would typically find attractive. He's tall – taller than Kieren if I had to guess. His shoulders are broad, the way he carries himself is statuesque, and I can tell by the stretch of the suit jacket sleeves around his arms that the fabric can barely contain his bulging muscles underneath.

I wouldn't be surprised to hear that he plays a sport like football or rugby, or that he's a descendant of the Vikings. Nor would I be surprised to see that the material of his pants can barely contain the husky girth of his thighs. Thinking of his thighs makes my mouth go dry, and I'm grateful for the presence of the ground-length tablecloth blocking my view of his lower half because otherwise, my intrusive thoughts would probably win, and I'd humiliate myself even more by gawking.

"So, I take it you're a freshman," he states, unphased by my ramble.

I gather myself and manage a nod. "I am. CS major, which, to be honest, I'm regretting."

He huffs a laugh. "Dornell's School of Engineering is notoriously tough. I'm a history major."

"What do you do with that after graduation?" I blurt out. *Fuck, that sounded rude.*

"Go to law school," he responds matter-of-factly.

"Of course," I realize, annoyed at my own ignorance. "That makes sense."

"That's the plan, anyway," he adds. "Graduate a year early and start at Stanford Law School next fall."

I blink, surprised and a bit self-conscious, if I'm being honest. He's going to graduate in three years and I'm struggling to pass my classes. God, I hate feeling so incredibly inadequate at this school.

"Where are you from?" he asks, pulling me from my whorl of insecurity.

Inwardly cringing, I brace for another one of these conversations designed to snuff out how wealthy my family is, how elitist I am, and whether I'm worth their time.

"Long Island, but I moved to Ohio when I was twelve," I rattle off.

"Huh. I'm from Michigan. I guess that makes us rivals," he grins.

Ah, yes. The college football rivalry comment. I press my lips together, anticipating the line of questioning I've received from nearly every single man on this campus when I tell them where I'm from.

"You're from Ohio? How much do you hate Michigan?"

"You're from Ohio? You must love college football, right?"

It makes me want to scream.

I take a sip from my wine glass without looking at Knox. "Yep. I guess that makes us rivals."

"You hate it when people say that, don't you?" he asks with a wry smirk.

"No. I love it," I banter sarcastically, feeling a scant amount of my confidence return.

He chuckles. "Well, for what it's worth, they say it to me, too. And I also find it annoying."

"I'm surprised," I let slip, instantly regretting my remark.

He cocks his head at me. "Surprised at what?"

I shake my head and simultaneously turn away while trying to wave off my comment.

"That I find it annoying when people ask me if I hate *The* Ohio State?" he presses.

Huffing, I turn to face him. Now I'm the one who's stereotyping.

"Yeah, I mean, you just look like you'd be into college football, is all." God, I sound like a fucking asshole. What did I just insinuate?

He gives me a knowing smile, takes a sip of his drink, then looks away.

"Sorry, maybe that was rude," I stammer. "I didn't mean for it to come off that way."

His grey-blue eyes hold mine. "Are you trying to say I look like a dumb jock?" he smiles playfully.

"No! No, not at all. And not all jocks are dumb. And not all people who like college football are dumb. Or jocks. I mean, you got into Dornell, you're obviously not stupid." I'm spinning now, desperate, but the hole I've dug gets deeper with each word that leaves my mouth.

He grins and leans forward, our eyes level. "You're making it worse," he whispers.

Oh God! He's right!

Every inch of my body floods with heat, and I don't have to look at my chest to know it's turned the color of a tomato. I have to flee. I have to get out of here.

My eyes dart around the lawn as my mind frantically tries to piece together my next move. Sweat beads across the top of my lip, and I try to swipe it away covertly, although I know there is nothing covert about the sweat now running down my temples.

"Monroe," he says, placing a gentle hand on my shoulder, "I'm just kidding."

I cling to his gaze, lost in his depthless eyes, when I hear, "What the fuck is going on?"

I jump backward at the sound of Kieren's angry voice, and feel my center become off balance as the heels of my stilettos sink into the soft grass. My drink tips, spilling everywhere, as I grapple with the tablecloth for purchase. Just when I thought this situation couldn't get more mortifying, it does.

"Whoa, don't fall!" Jace exclaims, grabbing the tops of my arms as I teeter backward. Jace presses me upright, and I have seconds to dislodge my heels from the soil before an infuriated Kieren is upon us. I can only imagine what he saw – Knox leaning down close enough to kiss me, and me doing not a damn thing to stop him.

11
MONROE

"What the fuck, Knox?" Kieren spits, bounding toward us. His venom draws confused and uncomfortable glares from the crowd.

Kieren stops inches from a seemingly unbothered Knox. My heart pounds as I watch Kieren's fingers curl at his sides. I hold my breath, expecting fists to fly. *Oh God, Kieren please don't. Knox will flatten you.* Tension radiates from Kieren like a furnace. Oppressive stares from onlookers crawl across my skin.

"Control yourself," Knox scolds with icy calm.

"Why were you touching her?" Kieren demands through a clenched jaw.

Knox doesn't answer. Instead, his steely blue eyes size up Kieren with playful amusement like an invincible fighter daring his unhinged opponent to swing.

I stand frozen, not knowing what to do. Accusatory thoughts race through my head. *This is my fault. I caused this. I should step in. Do something.*

"Kieren, let's take it easy," Jace says, cautiously lowering his hand to Kieren's shoulder.

Without breaking eye contact with Knox, Kieren aggressively shrugs off Jace's hand.

I take a small step forward. In the background, Gabi whisper-shouts my name. Time stops. I have to do this. I'm the only one who can de-escalate the situation.

"Kieren," I say timidly, lightly grazing the back of his arm with my fingers. "Maybe we should go." Getting him out of here is the only solution I can conjure in the heat of the moment.

He whirls to look down at me. Fury and disgust flood his eyes, but I force myself to breathe. Trailing the tips of my fingers down the sleeve of his suit jacket, I find the smooth skin of his hand. I glide my fingertips across his palm and brazenly thread my fingers through his.

"Kieren, let's leave," I plead quietly. My brain fixates on enunciating each word with soft neutrality, attempting to calm him down.

"Fine." His response is cold in a way that screams of his anger. Large fingers crush mine as he concedes. He takes a step toward the direction of the house, dragging me along with him.

Chatter resumes from the lawn, growing distant as we ascend the steps of the back porch. Wood paneling thumps under my feet as I struggle to keep pace with Kieren's long strides. As soon as the hallway inside becomes devoid of any discernible voices, I know. I sense it will happen seconds before it does, like when the barometric pressure suddenly drops right before a tornado touches the ground.

Kieren yanks me forward, throwing my back against the wall.

"What the fuck was that?" he sneers, squeezing my cheeks

with his fingers and thumb. His palm cups my jaw with frightening strength. "Are you trying to make me look like a fool?" he snarls.

I shake my head as vigorously as his vice around my jaw will allow.

"Don't let me catch you doing shit like that again. Understand?"

I nod my agreement, willing myself to breathe, but I can't. His pupils, inky black and soulless, nearly drown out his deep brown irises. I'm too terrified to look at them, yet too fearful to look away.

Voices echo from farther down the hall, and awareness takes hold. He slowly releases me without dropping my gaze. My body shakes with adrenaline as an expression I can only describe as consciousness returns to his face. The voices grow louder now to the point of recognizable – Gabi, Jace, and someone else.

"Come on," he says, reclaiming my hand. I stumble forward, nearly tripping over my feet.

Kieren leads me through the front room and down the stone steps of Sigma's main entrance. We walk quickly along the pathway, and the back of my heels sting from where Gabi's black stiletto shoes have sliced into my skin. By the time we make it to Kieren's car, I'm fighting back tears of pain.

He opens the passenger door for me but makes a point to slam it shut once I'm inside. My chin drops to my chest, and every muscle in my face tenses to stall the release of tears, but it's no use. I can't stop the wave of emotion, the crippling dejection that has me hunched over in a ball and sobbing before Kieren can climb inside.

His door shuts, cutting us off from the rest of the world, but he doesn't immediately start the engine. I sense he's looking at me, but I can't bring myself to face him.

The engine roars to life, and Kieren manually shifts the car into gear without a word to me.

I hear the muffled sound of Kieren's name called from outside the car. Daring a glance, I see Knox approaching us as tires feverishly churn atop loose gravel, and Kieren's BMW launches forward. Quickly, I look away, mortified by what I've caused, and ashamed by what they all must think of me for openly flirting with another man.

I'm appalled with myself. I should have acted better.

My relationship with Kieren is over, isn't it? Over before it's even begun.

12
KIEREN

"We're here, Monroe," I say quietly as I grip her thigh and give it a light shake. The first hour of our drive was spent listening to Monroe oscillate between air-gasping sobs and soft whimpers. At one point, I thought I would have to pull off the highway because she started to hyperventilate.

Could I have reacted differently? Absolutely. But I left Monroe alone for all of thirty minutes, trusting her to handle herself, only to return to Knox leaning over the table, hand on her shoulder, seconds from kissing her. *What in the actual fuck, Monroe?*

And now the pivotal weekend I had orchestrated for the two of us is off to a disastrous start.

Initially, I had planned to get Monroe ready during the drive. I assumed she would leave the alumni mixer more than a bit tipsy, and the four-hour drive would give me ample time to tease her to the point of begging.

I wanted her soaked by the time we arrived. I wanted her so beside herself with need that she'd climb onto my lap like a demon possessed, rip my zipper open, and ride my dick like a pogo stick the moment I parked my car.

But right now, she's not horny or soaked or begging for it, but that will change. We might have a different starting point, but the endpoint remains unchanged.

I help a half-asleep Monroe from the car and scoop her into my arms. Eye makeup is smeared around her eyes from all the crying and wiping, but she still looks beautiful.

She doesn't need to wear such heavy makeup; I blame Gabi for that crime. Monroe's natural face has an innocence to it that makes me want to ruin her. Her deep blue eyes don't need to be rimmed with black eyeliner to look smoldering. Nor do her lips need to be smothered in gloss to look supple. The only thing Monroe needs to enhance her already perfect appearance is me.

Her tits do look good in this dress, however.

"You can put me down now," she says as we cross through the threshold of the front door. I set her down gingerly. When she removed her shoes in the car, I saw how bloody and raw the skin on the back of her heels had become, which made me inexplicably angry that she would do that to herself. Yet another issue I'll have to work around this weekend.

I flick on a few lights and watch her expression change as she takes in her surroundings. My childhood home in Connecticut is... large. Some might say palatial, thanks to the fortune my father makes each year as CEO of Hunt Wealth Management. Running a family business has its perks, and he wasted no time snatching the reins from my aging grandfather. The man hadn't even formally retired yet when my greedy father took over, practically tossing my poor grandfather out with the day's trash.

"Are you hungry? I can sort out dinner," I say.

"You can cook?" she asks, hopeful.

"No, but I can order us something." She seems dissatisfied with this answer.

"Can *you* cook?" I ask skeptically.

She scoffs, rolling her eyes as she pads further into the house. "Yes, I can *cook*," she says, throwing a look of annoyance over her shoulder. "I did most of the cooking when I lived with my grandmother."

I really did not plan on spending any time this weekend cooking. What a waste. But, this seems sentimental to Monroe, and I need her to feel comfortable, so I offer a compromise. "I doubt there is any food worth cooking in the fridge right now. My parents have been gone for the last week. How about I order tonight, and tomorrow, we can go pick up supplies at the market?"

"Sure," she says. "Whatever you want."

The family portraits and artwork lining the living room have caught her eye. I follow her across the carpet, glancing down at my phone while I scroll through delivery food options.

"Is this your grandfather?" she asks, pointing to a framed family photo on the wall.

I look up. "Yep, sure is."

"I can see the resemblance," she comments.

I nod. People tell me this often. We both have that ruthless look about us.

She pauses and turns toward me, her arms crossed meekly in front of her. "I'm sorry," she offers. "I promise we were only talking about college football. That's it," she shares, looking down at her feet.

"Yeah, well, it was pretty fucked up to catch my girlfriend flirting with another man."

Her apprehensive ocean-blue eyes glance up to meet mine. "Am I your girlfriend? Because we've been hooking up exclusively for the past month, or at least, I've been exclusive, but..."

She gnaws on the inside of her lower lip, letting the remainder of her concerns go unspoken.

“Isn’t it clear that you’re the only one, Monroe? How much more obvious can I be?” I exclaim. “We spend more nights together than alone, sharing the same bed. You think I would do that with someone who wasn’t my girlfriend?”

She shrugs and looks down at her feet again. “Sometimes I don’t think you like me very much,” she mumbles.

“Not when you’re flirting with other guys, I don’t.”

Her expression is pained, and fuck, is she going to start crying again?

“Monroe, I’m sorry,” I say, simply because I cannot tolerate another meltdown. “I saw you two together, and I lost it. I’m sorry you feel hurt by how I reacted.”

Closing the distance between us, I tilt her chin upward so she’s forced to hold my gaze. “Let’s start over,” I say with intentional softness. “I want us to have a good weekend. Let’s put whatever happened earlier behind us, okay?”

Her eyes dart away before her eyelids become heavy. “Okay,” she sighs.

“Come with me,” I say, taking her hand. The hallways of the house are unlit and carry that sense of solemn silence I remember from my younger years when my parents would leave me home alone with the nanny while they attended yet another charity fundraiser or bullshit gala.

I switch on the lights as I progress further down the main corridor and toward the wing I occupied while living here. I trust my room and all my belongings are untouched. They were when I came home last to pack before leaving for Dornell.

One of these days, I know I’ll come home to find my belongings gone and my area of the house converted into an in-home Pilates studio. My mom has threatened to do so since I received my Dornell admissions acceptance package, and I’m sure she'll make good on her promise once she tires of spending my father's money on designer handbags and expensive lunches with her girlfriends in Manhattan. She has a pretty good life, that woman.

Flipping on the lights and then instantly dialing down the dimmer because their harsh, white glow is fucking blinding, I see my room is just as it was, which is a relief. I don't need Mom stumbling upon some of my more controversial personal possessions quite so soon.

Sitting on my bed, I pat my thighs in indication. Monroe walks toward me, eyeing me timidly.

"Closer," I say as she hesitates. "Monroe, come here," I reprimand.

Christ, her anxiety never relents. You'd think after letting me explore every inch of her body with my tongue, she'd be more acquiescent by now. I reach for her wrists to pull her between my legs and run my hands up the sides of her black satin dress, now creased from hours spent seated in the car. Wrapping my arms around her waist, her lower abdomen sits flush against my lips, and the tension in her body begins to dissipate.

"Turn around," I say, moving my hands to her hips. A heartbeat of reluctance passes across her face before she slowly pivots. I reach for the back zipper of her dress and pull it down at a languid pace. Each inch has the fabric spreading further apart, causing the straps to topple over her shoulders. Once I have her fully unzipped, I glide my palms up the small of her back and lower the straps over her arms. One yank has the form-fitting dress off her body and on the floor.

"No underwear?" I observe in pleasant surprise.

"You could see the underwear lines through the material," she explains.

I tsk as my fingers trail down her spine. By the time I make it to the curve of her ass, I've lost all self-restraint. I fist both cheeks and squeeze. Fuck, I want to bite it – sink my teeth into it like a goddamn apple.

And then I do.

She squeals when my teeth press into her flesh, not hard enough to draw blood but hard enough to leave a mark, and I inhale the smell of her building arousal.

Releasing her ass, I push two fingers into the soft flesh of her pussy, and she chokes out a moan.

"I'm going to fuck this pussy tonight," I assert, plunging my fingers further inside her hot center. She rocks into the pressure, keeping pace with my undulating motion. "You want more, don't you? Your pussy's so greedy for me, isn't it, Monroe?"

"Yes," she breathes, yet I can hear the trace thoughts of uncertainty in her voice.

"I need to hear you say it, Monroe."

"Yes. Please," she groans as my fingers thrust into her soaked pussy. Her body wants this, but I cannot leave any room for doubt. She needs to submit, physically and mentally, to prove she's ready.

"Again, Monroe. Say it like you mean it. Convince me." My voice is demanding as she works her pussy against my fingers.

"Please, Kieren," she begs. "I want you. I want you to..."

She gasps as I shove a third finger up inside her, hinging forward to accommodate the force of my thrusts.

"That's it, baby. Let's stretch out this tight cunt so it's ready to swallow all of me."

Her groans have turned unabashed in volume. I hook my other arm around her waist, pulling her close enough to kiss the back of her ribcage as the fingers of my free hand find her clit.

"Fuck, baby," I croon at her body's response, and I cannot

wait another goddamn second. My dick needs to be inside her dripping pussy immediately before my fucking balls explode. She whimpers when I remove my fingers.

Buttons fly from my dress shirt as I rip it open and off my body. My shoes, pants, and boxer briefs are next. Hesitation flickers across her face as she watches me undress, but I don't give her the chance to reconsider before I'm sitting again, pulling her on top of me.

She places a knee on either side of my thighs with an uncertain look.

"That's right baby," I assure her as I fist my cock, ready to thrust inside her the second she's in position. The anticipation of this moment, of finally fucking her, has my cock straining with need. My balls already ache for release, and glistening beads of precum dribble from the tip.

I guide my cock down her soaked slit until the head is aligned with her entrance. The walls of her pussy stretch as I push inside, molding around me in a euphoric squeeze like her body was custom-made for my size, and for once, I am fucking speechless.

Her breath hitches as I cautiously drive deeper inside her perfect pussy, careful not to move too fast or this will become the shortest fuck of my life.

My eyes open – I didn't even realize I had closed them – to see her face marred with anxiety, like she's on the verge of tears.

I stop even though my balls scream at me to keep going.

"Does it hurt?" I ask.

"No," she manages on an exhale. Her breasts rise and fall in rapid succession, but the rest of her body is rigid as she squeezes her eyes shut.

"Then what's wrong?" I push, trying not to get frustrated.

Are we honestly back here again? If she would just fucking relax, I could take care of her.

"Look at me, Monroe," I demand.

She opens her eyes, and fuck, I forgot that this girl is so goddamn innocent, like a fucking angel just begging to be corrupted in every single way imaginable.

It takes me a moment to gather myself, to remember how precious her vulnerability feels. How precious it felt when I touched her, tasted her, felt her pussy quiver for the first time. She'd never had an orgasm before, and I have to remind myself how fucking good it felt to know I was the first person to make her come. To taste it.

I can't explain the high it gave me to have such control over another human. None of my past experiences could hold a candle to what I felt that first time with Monroe. Almost as if I had extracted a piece of her soul that day and swallowed it down like a fucking god. Her body is a brilliant heat that I have now tethered to my darkness, and I will never, ever let this perfect creature go.

"Do you trust me?" I ask, gazing into her eyes with reassurance.

"Yes," she breathes.

"And do you trust me to give you what you need?" I press my thumb against her clit and gently circle.

"Yes," she says with a breathy moan.

"Then I need you to be a good girl, Monroe, and fucking take it."

My words come out gritty and harsh as I begin to buck my hips slowly. A pink flush blooms across her chest as she finds her rhythm.

"Good, baby. So good," I praise through clenched teeth.

Heavy-lidded eyes hold my gaze, but her expression tells

me her thoughts are still trapped elsewhere, and I can't let her self-consciousness go on any longer.

Palming her ass cheek, I pull her closer until my lips skim the crook of her neck. I drag my tongue along the distinct curvature of her collarbone until I reach the pocket of indentation where the shoulder connects with the socket and bite.

Gasping, she tries to pull away, but the hand I have on her backside holds her in place. Some of the women I've been with would end things here – the ones who claim they're into pain play until it actually happens. But the ones who enjoy it, like I suspect Monroe does, come alive.

I bite harder, knowing it may bruise, but the way Monroe has thrown her head back, moaning and riding my dick like a caged animal set free, tells me to keep going.

My balls constrict at the sight of her, and I know my own release is seconds from exploding.

Wrapping my index finger and thumb around her swollen clit, I gently pinch to increase the pressure on either side of her bud.

"Kieren," she wails.

I pinch harder, adding pain to the mix of friction.

"Kieren, I'm..."

More words aren't needed. I know she's going to come when I feel her inner walls tent, strangling my dick. Groaning against her skin, my saliva turns to drool as I squeeze my eyes shut. I have dreamed of her tight little cunt milking me dry from the moment I met her.

Her breath hitches as release crashes through her core. Her pussy spasms and contracts around my cock, and the feeling is fucking ecstasy. My ears ring with the sound of her screams, and my eyes must have rolled to the back of my head because I swear, I black out. I can't remember the last time I waited this long to fuck a woman.

But Monroe...

Monroe was worth it.

My balls echo Monroe's release with their own, flooding her with a firehose of cum, and she's so full that our orgasms have converged into an overflowing river now running down my inner thighs.

Goddamn, this woman is heroin.

I dislodge my mouth from her skin like a suction cup. Sunken, blueish-purple teeth marks form two semicircles around swollen red skin. Her forehead rests against mine; her arms are wrapped around the back of my neck, as our chests rise and fall in unison. I run my hands over the smooth skin of her back as I nuzzle her neck.

"How do you feel?" I ask, craning my neck backward so I can see her eyes. Her dark blue irises are muddled with emotion – confounded and glassy. I can see her mind struggle to understand her body's reaction to being both bitten and pinched, thinking perhaps it should have felt wrong. But it didn't. It felt like fucking rapture because otherwise, she wouldn't have erupted three seconds later.

"Good," she mutters meekly, then looks away.

"Monroe," I say firmly, grabbing her chin between the same two fingers that had pinched her clit sixty seconds ago. "Use your words. Tell me. How do you feel?"

Her throat works as she swallows.

"I feel...," she begins, then stops as if afraid to answer.

"You feel?" I ask again. "You're not moving until you tell me."

Admittedly, the thought of another round causes my now flaccid penis to twitch back to life. She shifts her hips in response, likely feeling me stiffen inside her.

"I feel like my body's been asleep my entire life," she admits. "And it just woke up."

13
MONROE

Angry blueish-brown skin stares back at me in the mirror. Teeth marks are at the center of the bruised area where Kieren bit me last night. Should I feel frightened? My mind is stuck in a playback loop – the memory of the bite, the flash of pain, the flood of heat, followed by the most intense orgasm I've ever experienced. Granted, my depth of experience is severely limited, seeing as I've only been with Kieren for a month and change, and while he's always made me come, he's never made me come *like that.* I don't know what that says about me or my body. Does pain stimulation turn me on? I mean, clearly it does. But it's hard to wrap my head around what feels like a significant sexual awakening.

I have a feeling Kieren's just gotten started, because how else would you know to bite and pinch someone like that? He must have practiced those moves before to know that not only can administering pain heighten your partner's pleasure, but send them over the edge as well.

How far does this pain play ride go, exactly? What if I want to get off? *Do* I want to get off?

I woke up to an empty bed and a note in Kieren's scribbled handwriting letting me know he had stepped out to run errands and that I should make myself at home. I decided a shower would be a smart idea, but since I had no clothes with me, I searched Kieren's room until I found a pair of athletic shorts and T-shirt. Admittedly, I snooped a bit more because he did leave me home alone, but his room is spotless save for several large suitcases in his closet, which I didn't have the courage to rifle through. The only slightly concerning discovery was the sizable array of prescription medications I found in his bathroom. Adderall didn't surprise me, and neither did Lexapro or Xanax – I've heard of these medications before – but the mood stabilizers required an online search, which resulted in more questions than answers, not about Kieren, but about myself.

I've come to learn that Kieren is a complex individual, probably more complicated than I've yet to experience, but some of the symptoms these medications are meant to treat remind me a bit of myself.

An incoming call from Gabi pulls me from my online medical rabbit hole. Shit. I forgot to call her back. How long have I been standing in this bathroom?

"Hey," I answer in a nonchalant tone that surprises me since nothing about the last twenty-four hours has been nonchalant.

"Monroe, what the fuck, are you okay?" Gabi demands, launching straight into the heated confrontation I knew would happen. "I've been out of my mind worried about you! I called and texted you like fifty times!"

"I know. I know. I'm sorry. I lost track of time and last night was a blur."

"I'd say. What happened?! Did he hurt you? Are you in Connecticut?"

I wince at her barrage of questions. "Did it look that bad?" I grimace, remembering how we bolted from the alumni mixer in a blaze of Kieren's rage.

"Monroe!" Gabi scolds. "Kieren practically dragged you out of Sigma by your hair. Are you kidding me? You should have heard the earful Knox gave Jace after you two left."

"What did he say?" I ask curiously, trying to hide how eager I am to hear the answer.

"That Jace needs to stop acting like a pussy and put Kieren in his place. That he can't treat you like that. That he's going to make Kieren and Jace's lives absolute hell next semester when they pledge Sigma. That it's going to be so bad, Kieren will wish he were dead, and if he ever sees Kieren treat you like that again, he'll kill him himself."

"Oh wow," I whisper, more ashamed than stunned, because for a complete stranger to have such a visceral reaction to Kieren's behavior, it must have looked much worse than I remember. *God, I'm humiliated by my own ineptitude.*

"Yeah, it was intense. Do you know Knox? I mean, have you met him before?"

"No, never," I mutter. "I've seen him around Sigma at parties, but we've never formally met until yesterday."

"You two seemed like you were hitting it off before crazy Kieren ruined everything."

"We were just talking about being from Ohio and Michigan and college football. It was nothing. I don't know," I ramble. Had I been flirting with him? Truly, I didn't think I was, but it must have looked that way given Gabi's observation. Shit, no wonder Kieren was furious.

"Speaking of Kieren, what happened last night, Monroe?" Gabi presses, determined to know if he crossed the line.

"Nothing, I'm fine. I promise. We drove to Connecticut and I fell asleep in the car. When we got here, things were fine."

"*Things were fine*?" Gabi challenges.

"Yeah. We... we had sex," I say quickly, bracing myself for her judgment.

"Did he force you?" she asks, still livid.

"No. Definitely not. It was my choice. I wanted it to happen," I assure her.

"And? Was it okay? Jace said Kieren's into some heavy BDSM stuff. Did anything like that happen last night?"

"Not last night," I pause. "Well, maybe a little." Do biting and pinching count as BDSM? I frankly have no idea, but I'm not going to say this to Gabi, who is already on the warpath.

"It was honestly... incredible," I admit, hoping this eases her hostility toward Kieren. "It's hard to put into words how good it felt, Gabi. Mind-blowing, I guess people say?"

"Okay," she says, drawing out the word like she's questioning my sanity. "Well... Maybe you have an untapped freaky side."

I scoff a laugh. "Yeah, maybe."

The line goes quiet, both of us unsure what to say.

"I'm glad you're okay," Gabi says, breaking the silence. "I seriously was going to make Jace drive me to Connecticut to chop Kieren's dick off. It was not cool how he acted, Monroe."

"I know," I acknowledge.

"Please *call me* or at least text me this weekend to let me know you're okay."

"I will," I promise. "Thank you Gabi. I'll be fine though, I swear."

"Yeah, famous last words," she jokes.

"Oh, shoot. Jace just texted me that he's downstairs. We're going to brunch, so I have to run, but love you!" she adds cheerfully, then ends the call.

I stare at the black screen, cradling the phone in my hand before setting it down on the counter.

"Love you," she had said. I know it was just a friendly sign off to the call, an off-the-cuff comment, tossed in with the rest of her words. Yet, to me, it was everything.

Maybe it's because no one says those words to me. My grandmother had now and then, but a friend? To be loved by a friend? To have someone care enough to be concerned? Tears well in the corners of my eyes, and I am overwhelmed by a profound sense of belonging.

I matter to someone – someone who is not my grandmother. Someone who wasn't ordered by the courts and Child Protective Services to give a shit.

I fucking matter.

14
MONROE

The smart home deadbolt squeals open, jolting me from my scrolling session. It's almost noon, and I'm on my third Nespresso coffee. Kieren practically skips into the kitchen, seemingly in a good mood, carrying shopping bags.

"Got us food for later," he says, setting the brown paper grocery bag on the counter. "You can cook steak, right?" he asks with a wink.

I scoff. "Yeah, I actually can," I respond. "Can you, Mr. '*I grew up with a private chef?*'"

"Of course," he smirks, but I highly doubt he's so much as boiled water.

"I also got you clothes," he adds, setting the second shopping bag in front of me.

"How kind of you, considering you practically kidnapped me. You could have just told me your plan, you know? Then I could have packed a bag and brought my makeup."

"We can buy you makeup, Monroe, if it makes you feel better. Do you want to do that?"

"You're the one who has to look at my face without makeup all weekend."

He levels me a glare. "You don't need makeup," he says as he wedges between my legs for a kiss. My arms wrap around the nape of his neck, and the edge of the kitchen counter digs into the small of my back.

"I like you in my clothes." I feel his smile against my lips, and it makes me giggle.

"What's so funny?" he continues.

"You," I flirt, as I kiss him.

He growls in displeasure against my mouth, which only causes me to laugh harder. Before I can register the movement, Kieren lifts me from the stool and slings me over his shoulder.

"Put me down!" I laugh. His free hand yanks down the waistband of his shorts that are already sagging off my small frame and smacks my ass with enough force to leave a welt. I yelp in pain, wincing at the lingering sizzle of his palm against my skin as he carries me down the long hallway toward his bedroom.

I'm flung unceremoniously onto the bed, and the startle of the mattress against my back knocks the air from my lungs. I open my mouth, but before I can get a word out, he's on top of me, and I'm pinned in place by his thighs.

"This can go one of two ways. You can obey like a good girl and get rewarded, or you can fight and get punished. The choice is yours, Monroe. Do you understand?"

"Wh… What?" I choke, caught off guard. His eyes glimmer with wicked malice, and I can't tell if he's joking or serious.

In one blink, Kieren has both my nipples clamped between his fingers. A searing pain bursts across my chest, up my neck, and spears down my center. I gasp as tears pool at the outer corners of my eyes.

"Already disobedient. You're not off to a good start, Monroe. Try again," he says in a low growl.

He repeats himself, and immediately, I answer. "Yes, I understand."

My bowed back relaxes down to the mattress in relief as he releases my nipples.

"Do. Not. Move," he instructs; each word punctuated. He climbs off me, and I feel the bed spring up at the loss of weight. I can hear him unzip something on the other side of the room, and my heart begins to race. Rustling noises and clinking sounds send my mind into a state of panic. The tips of my fingers begin to quiver, and my breathing turns erratic. *Is this the BDSM stuff Gabi mentioned or is he going to kill me?*

"Whatever you're thinking, stop thinking it," Kieren commands from across the bedroom.

Is my fear that obvious? My legs and arms splay out like a starfish as I gaze at the ceiling. His oversized T-shirt is hiked over my breasts, and I have to actively fight the urge to pull it down. I've watched enough crime dramas to know how this game works.

I hear him approach the bed and make the mistake of turning my head to look. I manage to get the words, "*Kieren, what are you*," out of my mouth before his knees sink to either side of my ribcage, and he silences me with his hand.

"What did I tell you?" he asks in a deep, guttural voice I'm not sure I've heard him use before.

"Open," he says, uncovering my mouth.

Hesitantly, I part my lips.

"Wider, puppy," he says. Slowly, I open my mouth like I would at the dentist.

"Good. Now keep it open."

My eyes flick back up to the ceiling, and that's when I see something black headed straight for my face. I buck at the intrusion of what feels like a silicone ball gag in my mouth, but I quickly realize it's not just a ball gag. Smooth material that I'm pretty sure is leather cups my chin and encases my cheeks. The bottom half of my face is completely covered.

It's like a... It's like a muzzle.

It is *a fucking muzzle!*

Awareness has my eyes flaring open. I attempt to say something, but all that comes out is an incoherent whine.

"Sit up," Kieren commands as he repositions himself behind me on the bed. I fumble to push myself into a seated position. My heart pounds in my chest, struggling to take in oxygen, like being forced to breathe only through my nose might suffocate me. But part of me feels... enthralled. I'm sitting in the front seat of a rollercoaster as it ascends – terrified, flushed with heat, yet ripe with anticipation of the thrill.

Kieren tugs at the straps of this thing, and I brace myself as the restriction of the muzzle gets tighter.

"There," Kieren coos with delight like he's so damn proud of himself.

Kieren's fingertips skim the sides of my stomach as he lifts the T-shirt over my head. I raise my arms in surrender as the cotton fabric slips off.

Saliva has started to run from my mouth and pool at the base of the muzzle, and I can't decide if I should be embarrassed by this or if it's par for the course.

"Lie back down," Kieren instructs with his palm pressed against my sternum. He straddles my ribcage again as he lifts my right hand. Smooth leather similar to that of the muzzle wraps around my wrist.

Cinch.

My left wrist.

Cinch.

The thick leather cuffs press into my skin to the point of

discomfort. This day has taken an unexpected turn. How did I go from having sex all of three times in my life to wearing a muzzle? Was last night just a trial run for the main event? Jesus, this is insane. Absolutely insane. But, fuck, the throbbing demand between my legs is overwhelming.

I can't feel the muzzle anymore, or the gag, or the wrist restraints, because all I can feel is a building frenzy in my core, and Kieren hasn't even fucking touched me yet.

My thoughts churn, the pulsing need at my center becomes desperate, as Kieren pulls off the shorts I'm wearing and wraps each ankle with similar restraints to those around my wrists.

"Almost done, puppy. I must say, you're behaving so well. I expected more fight, but I guess you're a good little pet after all."

I don't hear his twisted praise. All I hear is the sound of clips opening and closing, followed by the harrowing sound of chain metal. My breath turns ragged when my legs are forced into a wide spread as Kieren secures each leg to the lower corners of the bed. When he secures the last restraint and I realize I'm fully immobilized, true panic takes hold.

The back of my throat works to enunciate his name, even though all that comes out are mangled grunts. I am completely naked and more vulnerable than I've ever been in my life.

"What's wrong, puppy? You don't like this?" he tuts in a tone laced with cruel amusement.

When I shake my head vigorously, he crawls on top of me until his face is directly above mine. His dark pupils are lust-blown, and his lips are quirked upward in a sinister smirk.

"Aww, well that's too bad, because the fun part is just beginning."

I whimper, pleading with my eyes, and then his face disappears from view.

"See, I thought it would be fun to try a little experiment."

I hold my breath in rapt attention, petrified.

"An experiment where we try new things," he explains. A clamping sensation crushes my right nipple, and I cry in protest. But I don't just feel the clamp. I feel a string – no, a wire – skimming atop my chest and down across my abdomen. Then comes the second clamp on my left nipple. I jerk at the wrist restraints, but it's no fucking use.

"Let's give these a quick test, shall we?"

I scream against the gag as the most insane stimulation I've ever felt careens through my body. My toes curl into the bedsheets, the only grip I can manage, as tiny stinging needles of vibrating pain burst across my breasts. And for some fucked up reason I cannot comprehend, I also feel dull tickles of vibration in my clit.

Holy fuck, I realize. He's hooked my nipples up to some sort of electric shock kink machine.

I can barely catch my breath, because I felt that... *everywhere*.

"Mmm, great, those work," Kieren hums in satisfaction. "It's an electrostimulation toy, by the way, but you've probably surmised as much. It's not intended to cause real pain – only mild electrical pulses to stimulate muscles and nerves."

Not intended to cause real pain, my ass, I think.

My eyes must look crazed because Kieren's fingertips caress my temple. "Shhh, it's all part of your training, Monroe. You need to learn how to be my good little puppy, because, see, *I've claimed you*. I fucked you last night and filled your pussy with my cum, remember? No one else gets to have you. Not anymore. No more flirting with other guys. You're mine now."

Pathetic whimpers catch in my throat as his psychotic grin and equally unhinged words snake around my mind. Yesterday, I was scared he would leave me. Losing him was a possibility I couldn't fathom. I want him, all of him, and it seems my wish was granted, because now, there's no turning back. An image of what I must look like from above bursts to the forefront of my mind. Even though I'm naked, vulnerable, and chained to his teenage bed, with my nipples hooked up to an electric shock machine like I'm fucking Frankenstein's bride, the relief I feel to know I'm his is undeniable.

"Don't worry, you'll like this next surprise, I promise," he says with vicious mockery. His fingers spread my labia. I hold my breath. A sharp pressure compresses my clit, and then I realize my fate.

"Now, we know the nipple ones work," Kieren says matter-of-factly, and I can't tell if he's talking to me or an imaginary friend. "But, we still need to test the clit."

I scream-moan into the ball gag as my back arches involuntarily. Intense, vibrating pain shocks my core. Kieren switches off the stimulation a second later, and even though the sensation was jarring, my pussy started to immediately quiver. I bear down on the ball gag because fuck, I think I nearly came. I squirm on the bed, groaning.

"Perfect. You're such a well-behaved puppy, Monroe," Kieren praises. "I think you've earned a reward."

I wail loudly in protest because, given my current circumstances, Kieren's definition of reward might not be so rewarding. The end of the bed sags with Kieren's weight, and I feel him slide what I assume is a soft towel under my ass.

"Goddamn, I wish you could see how glistening wet your pussy is right now, puppy." My breath hitches when his fingers graze my entrance and circle. "I wish you could see how greedy your little cunt looks spread open like this." He makes a noise that sounds like the type of elongated growl you make when biting into something exceptionally delicious. "I want to watch you come," he groans.

A heartbeat of silence passes, and then the clit stimulation starts again. My shoulder blades dig into the bed. My ribcage bows open. The build of an orgasm happens so fast that I come in seconds.

"Fuck," Kieren growls in admiration as my orgasm hurtles down my pulsing pussy like a fucking freight train. My cheeks under the muzzle are slick with sweat. I yank at the wrist restraints as I writhe my ass against the bed. My core is on fire and my pussy is throbbing. I have never felt this turned on before – this *needy*. I *need* the pressure of penetration or my pussy is going to fucking explode.

A stifled scream of frustration rasps up my throat. The sound is pitiful.

I squeeze my eyes together and huff through my nose. Kieren's amused chuckle stokes my fury, and I lift my head to give him my most pissed off glare.

"I'm going to unpack the groceries," he begins coolly in a tone that is infuriatingly unbothered. "But don't worry, I have an app on my phone that controls the e-stim intensity, so I can play with you while I'm gone. It's like one of those treat-dispensing machines pet owners use to reward their dogs while they're away," he says, giddy.

I try to curse at Kieren, but my words are comically ineffective. Kieren kneels on the right side of the bed, smirking down at me with amusement. "I expect to see a puddle under your ass large enough to splash in with rainboots by the time I get back, puppy," he says in a low rasp, stroking my hair.

He leans down, his lips feather my right earlobe, and whispers, "I want you more soaked and swollen than you've ever been in your life because I plan to fuck you on all fours like an absolute savage. I'm going to drive my dick so far up your tight little cunt, it'll rearrange your insides."

The thought of getting fucked so brutally and rough elicits an unintentional moan, and I can feel his vicious smile against my ear. God, I shouldn't want this as badly as I do, yet both my mind and body are thrumming with a perverse, burning desire to be absolutely ruined.

"When I come back in this room, I want you in tears for this dick. Do we have an understanding?"

I can barely manage a nod because I'm shaking so badly with adrenaline that I'm on the verge of convulsing.

"Good," he says, pleased. "Because there is nothing I want more than to watch my sweet puppy beg."

15
MONROE

Winter Break, Freshman Year,
Dornell University

"It's not too late," Gabi says as she zips her suitcase.

"Unfortunately, I think it is," I respond.

Gabi huffs a sigh. "You know, Kieren's in for a rude awakening next semester when he pledges Sigma and you and I join a sorority. He won't be able to whisk you away every other weekend to Connecticut."

I press my lips together as I nod.

"I mean, I get it. He's in love with you, or whatever," Gabi rattles off. "But he's still on my shit list."

"He's not in love with me," I interject.

"Please. He's told you he loves you, hasn't he?" she asks.

"No," I scoff. "Why? Has Jace told you he loves you?"

A grin creeps across Gabi's face.

"He has?!" I exclaim.

She shrugs to downplay her emotions, but she's beaming from ear to ear. "Yeah, a lot actually," she admits.

"When did this start?" I ask in disbelief. Maybe I'm awestruck because, despite regularly fucking me into oblivion, Kieren hasn't so much as said a word about serious feelings. Maybe I should find this concerning? We manage to share a bed most nights of the week, but because so much of our relationship is driven by sex, I feel like I barely know him even after three months.

Gabi chews on her bottom lip. "Honestly, after the first few weeks. He said, 'I don't want to scare you off, but I'm falling in love with you.' And I told him I felt the same way, and then it was just... out there. We say it to each other all the time now."

My face has gone slack with envy. "Oh," I swallow. A rush of anxiety floods my nerves, and suddenly, I feel lightheaded. I'm no fool to think my relationship with Kieren is normal. I don't think other Dornell girls my age are chained up and fucked like depraved animals on the weekend by their boyfriends. I doubt other Dornell girls are putting on BDSM paraphernalia and having back-to-back, intense orgasms that have literally caused a temporary loss of consciousness.

But, still. Should he love me, or at least, like me enough to tell me I mean more to him than kinky sex?

The thought that Kieren might not have feelings for me beyond lust makes me feel sick to my stomach. Given how much we fuck, I just assumed he did, but now, I'm not so sure. Have I been a fool this entire time?

Nausea churns inside my gut. Now I really regret agreeing to go to Kieren's birthday dinner tomorrow. This already felt like a stretch, because I have to drive with Kieren to New York City tomorrow, go to his birthday dinner, then take the bus back to Dornell the following morning to get my car and drive back to Ohio. Flights were too expensive and therefore, not an option.

"Sorry, I shouldn't have said anything," Gabi says, sensing my unease. "Every couple is different. Don't think about the timing, Monroe. I'm sure Kieren loves you, but just needs more time to say it out loud. This is a very normal thing. Jace is the abnormal one."

"It's fine," I say and force an awkward smile.

"Okay, but like I said, it's not too late," Gabi says, returning to her earlier comment. "You can still go with Kieren to the Swiss Alps."

I shake my head. "In no world can I afford a trip that lavish. Plus, I can't ski, and I really want to see my grandmother. I told you she seemed worse when I saw her over Thanksgiving."

"But you can do both," Gabi protests.

"Gabi, I am broke. Do you remember the part where I told you I'm here only because of financial aid? Even then, I had to take out a student loan. I'll probably find some part-time work for a few weeks while I'm home for the holiday so I can afford gas."

"Just let Kieren pay for you! It's the least he can do to make up for the times he acted like a dick this past semester," she exclaims, as if that option is so easy. "Didn't he offer?"

"Absolutely not," I say, almost offended. "We're not talking a few hundred dollars for a plane ticket. We're talking tens of thousands of dollars. The thought of Kieren paying my way for the entire trip makes me deeply uncomfortable."

She tosses a few more pieces of makeup into her bag.

"I get it. It would make me uncomfortable, too. I'm only suggesting it because he got so upset when you told him you couldn't go."

Unreasonably upset, I think. His reaction felt exceedingly disproportionate.

Sighing, I say, "Hopefully me going to his birthday dinner will be enough, but truthfully, I'm dreading it. I wish you and Jace were going. I still can't believe you're bringing him home to meet your parents."

"I know," Gabi agrees. "I'm a bit terrified. My dad is...," she pauses, shaking her head as she searches for the right words. Gabi's mentioned her strained relationship with her father, so I can only imagine how nervous she must be.

"I just hope it doesn't end in some explosive disaster," she says. "But, my mom is thrilled. Shit, she'll probably get here any minute," Gabi curses, checking the time on her phone. "She called this morning to say she left the real estate broker conference early and is now driving here as we speak."

"Wait, I just got a text from her. Dammit, she's twenty minutes away! I need to text Jace. I'm sure the birthday dinner won't be as bad as you're expecting," Gabi says offhandedly as she rushes to finish packing.

"It's all his Andover friends whom I've never met. I'm sure they're all elitist, rich kids like Kieren, and I can't shake this nervousness in the pit of my stomach that this dinner will feel like the first week of Dornell all over again," I groan. All I want to do is hide under the blankets.

"Don't let those snobby, arrogant assholes get to you, Monroe. You are so much better than they are, and besides, you've already stolen the heart of the most arrogant asshole I've ever met. This dinner will be a walk in the park," she assures me.

I roll my eyes. "I'm going to miss you," I sigh. "Text me updates, okay? I need to know if Jace survives your dad's interrogation."

"And to plan our outfits for sorority rush," Gabi adds with a saucy grin.

"If you say so," I say with a shake of my head.

“I know you’re secretly excited,” Gabi adds.

I chuckle. “It’s true,” I admit. I never had many friends growing up, especially not after moving to Ohio, so the thought of being accepted into an organization that calls itself a sisterhood is thrilling. “Watch me be president one day,” I jest.

“You’d make a great president,” Gabi smiles. “I bet you’ll run unopposed.”

This makes me grin. “What makes you think that?”

“Because if anyone tries to run against you, I’ll shank them.”

She says this with such nonchalance that I burst out laughing.

“What?” Gabi asks, looking earnestly perplexed. “It’s me and you against the world, baby. If they want to come for you, they’ve got to go through me first.”

16

MONROE

Winter Break, Freshman Year,
New York City

"Name?" the hostess asks.

"Helena Yates," Kieren responds.

"Right this way," the hostess immediately responds without glancing at the reservation list. My brows crinkle together. Kieren told me nothing about this birthday dinner other than several of his Andover friends will be in attendance. I assume Helena is one of these said friends, although in my mind, I had taken friends to mean those of the same sex. Clearly, I was wrong.

I reach for Kieren's hand as we follow the hostess, but he pulls away. I had sensed his mood was off from the moment I climbed into his car at Dornell. He told me nothing was wrong when I asked, but he seemed to get increasingly agitated the closer we got to Manhattan. After spending most of the drive in uncomfortable silence, we checked into the hotel Kieren had booked for the night, quickly changed, and then left for dinner.

Tables packed with diners chatter around us as we weave through the restaurant. The interior ambiance is dimly lit, creating an aura of intrigue and mystery. I can't help but glance at the softly illuminated faces of the surrounding patrons because this seems like the type of place famous people would frequent. We had to pass through a large velvet curtain when we arrived, and the plush leather booths and dark wood furniture made me think we'd walked into a speakeasy. Wall sconces bathe the dining room with gentle light, and I can't help but admire the glittering, low-hanging chandeliers.

Suddenly, shouts of birthday wishes make my heart flutter as the hostess steps to the side.

"Kieren!"

"There he is!"

"Finally, the birthday boy has arrived!"

"Fashionably late as always!"

Everyone talks at once, and I watch awkwardly from the sidelines as Kieren is engulfed by a frenzy of hugs and back slaps. Finding the courage to plaster a forced smile across my face, I inch closer. Multiple two and four-person tables have been pushed together to create one long table in the center of the restaurant, and as I take in the faces of those already seated around the table, my stomach sinks. There must be fifteen people here, but I only recognize one person, Barrett, from the Sigma parties, and he's not someone I know well.

The end of the table where I stand has resumed conversation, so I timidly approach the opposite end where Kieren is engrossed in what seems to be the most entertaining of discussions with a chestnut-haired woman. Her outfit is immaculate. I spot not one designer logo on her clothes, yet I'm sure her outfit costs more than a year of my tuition. The black Birkin bag resting haphazardly on the maroon leather booth, like she simply tossed it aside upon arrival, is not lost on me.

I stand near her, like a fish out of water, and wait for Kieren to remember I'm here and introduce me. He doesn't. Only when she senses the presence of a body lingering beside her does she turn.

"Hi," I say uneasily when our eyes meet, "I'm Monroe."

She blinks in confusion before Kieren jumps in and says, "Helena, this is Monroe. Monroe, this is Helena. She's one of my friends from Andover."

Helena clucks and jabs Kieren with her elbow. "*One of your friends?* Is that all I am to you, Cunty?"

Cunty? Did I hear her correctly?

Kieren playfully rolls his eyes. "Okay, fine. One of my dearest and oldest friends. We've known each other since childhood."

"Cunty and I used to play in each other's backyards growing up," she says with a charmed grin. "We were neighbors for a bit before he ditched me for that monstrosity of a house in the next town over. Do your parents still live there?" she asks, returning to Kieren.

The restaurant is loud, and I can barely hear Kieren's response.

"Here, sit!" she exclaims, motioning to the open space adjacent to the seat she's claimed at the head of the table. I walk around her, removing my coat, and shimmy myself down the leather booth. I situate myself as best I can while Kieren sidles next to me. I can feel the stares of those seated across from us.

"I'm Monroe," I say, and offer the couple a friendly wave. They tell me their names, but I immediately forget, distracted by the loud ruckus of conversation happening all around me. I reach for my water glass and take a sip. This is so goddamn painful.

"How do you know Kieren?" the girl directly across from me asks. I lean forward, straining to hear her.

"From Dornell. I'm his girlfriend," I say loudly.

Helena whips her head toward me, then back to Kieren with a look of shock.

"Kieren, this is your *girlfriend*? Why are you hiding her from us?" she chides. "We don't bite!"

Kieren sips from the champagne glass placed in front of him after he sat down.

"Please," he scoffs. "You all are animals."

"Miriam, this is Kieren's girlfriend!" Helena shouts down the table. The woman who must be Miriam returns Helena's look of shock.

"Kieren! You never said anything!" Miriam shouts.

"That's what I said!" Helena shouts back. "He's hiding her from us! He said we're all animals and we'd corrupt her!" Helena grins wickedly.

"Us? Never!" Miriam shouts, chasing her response with a gulp of champagne.

"Did I hear you call him Cunty?" I ask, leaning forward. I latch on to this opportunity to integrate myself into the conversation.

Helena giggles and gives Kieren an endearing look.

"Kieren loves the nickname. Don't you, Cunty?"

Kieren downs the rest of his champagne. "I'd have thought you'd come up with something more creative by now," Kieren chides.

"Nope," Helena smirks. "Cunty is here to stay."

"His last name is Hunt, and, well, you get the idea," she says, winking at me. "I couldn't help myself. I've called him Cunty since secondary school. Girls are much more clever with the insults, you know. Even at a young age. You poor boys just can't keep up."

He grumbles something and pours another glass of champagne.

"To the birthday boy!" Helena toasts, and the table erupts in cheer.

Plates of food begin to arrive, and admittedly, I'm starved, but apparently so is the rest of the table because they descend on the food like vultures. Various dishes make their rounds. I spoon leaves of well-dressed lettuce on my plate along with pasta that smells like fancy mac-and-cheese. More dishes are brought to the table – large round bowls filled with oysters and caviar nestled in ice, massive charred steaks that smell like the heavens, and sides of creamed spinach and mushrooms. It's a feast.

Rounds of espresso martinis land around the table along with a whiskey Kieren ordered, but without a fake I.D., I'm too nervous to attempt a cocktail order, so the champagne will have to do. Kieren has hardly uttered a word to me since sitting. I skim his thigh with my fingertips to get his attention when Barrett shouts Kieren's name from the opposite end of the table.

"Kieren, look who it is!"

Kieren shakes his head, and I look around the dining room in curiosity.

"Of all the fucking places," Kieren shouts back.

I lean into Kieren and ask, "Who is it?"

"No one," he answers tersely without looking at me and downs the remainder of his whiskey.

"What's wrong?" I ask, pressing into him. "Is everything okay?"

He makes eye contact with a waiter and taps his empty glass. I've lost track of how many drinks Kieren has had. I know it's his birthday and he wants to celebrate, but I've rarely seen him have more than one or two drinks.

"Maybe you should have some water," I suggest, moving his untouched glass closer. He grumbles something under his breath.

"What?" I ask, and it comes out louder and harsher than I intended.

He turns into me, grabbing my forearm to yank me closer. The movement happens so fast, it catches me by surprise, and I accidentally utter a clipped yelp. Eyes, including Helena's, flick our direction.

"I said, don't tell me what to do," he growls against my ear and then lets go. I swallow my silence and pretend the last five seconds didn't happen.

"Kieren," Helena begins, slicing through the tension. "Where are you going for holiday?"

The waiter sets a fresh whiskey in front of Kieren, and I watch Helena motion something to him.

"The Alps," he responds.

"Oh my God, I love the Swiss Alps," Helena pines.

"You should come," Kieren says.

"Oh, no, I wouldn't want to crash your romantic getaway."

"Monroe's not coming," Kieren grumbles.

Helena makes an exaggerated gasping noise. "Monroe, you're not going? Do you not like the Alps?"

"I don't ski, unfortunately," I say.

"No," Kieren corrects me, annoyed. "You could *learn* how to ski, but that's not why."

Helena looks at me expectantly, and my voice is frozen in the back of my throat. How can I say the truth? And, in front of Kieren's friends, who are most definitely in the upper echelon of society. I can't. I'll humiliate myself.

So, instead, I say, "I want to spend the holidays with my

grandmother. She's very old and I'm not sure how much time she has left."

"Aww," Helena pouts. "That's so sweet. Kieren, your girlfriend is such a sweetheart, wanting to spend the holidays with her grandmother instead of getting drunk on the slopes with the rest of you degenerates."

Kieren gulps the last sip of his drink, and slams down his glass.

"Oh, I'll be right back," Helena proclaims to our end of the table in an obnoxiously giddy tone. "Need to help the waitstaff with something. Kieren, don't go anywhere!"

"What the fuck is your problem?" I hiss.

He clinks the remains of an ice cube around his empty glass.

"Why did you lie?" he bites back, his jaw clenched as he speaks.

"About what?" I gape. "About why I'm not going on the trip?"

I search his face, but he refuses to look at me.

"Would you rather I said I'm not going because I'm poor and can't afford to drop thousands of dollars on a lavish vacation?"

"It's my fucking birthday," he grits. "You should *want* to be with me."

I glance around to see if our hushed argument has drawn unwanted attention, but thankfully, the rest of the table is oblivious.

"Then you should have picked a different place," I snip. A bubble of anxiety rises in my throat as my pulse begins to race, and I sense the emotional control I've had up until this point start to slip.

He turns, and his eyes are livid. Rarely do I fight back, but

I've reached my breaking point, and now I can't stop myself from antagonizing him further.

"But Helena can go," I say sarcastically with a saccharine smile. "She simply loves the Alps," I add, pouting with blatant mockery.

He leans into me, and I wrinkle my nose at the overpowering smell of whiskey on his breath.

"Why do you think I've never let you meet my parents?" he says in a harsh rasp against my ear. "Why do you think they're conveniently never home when we're there? Why do you think no one at this table, outside of Barrett, knows about you?"

I pull back, searching his eyes for a semblance of humanity, because surely, he can't mean what I think he's implying. Surely, he can't be this elitist and disgusting to claim he hasn't introduced me to anyone because I'm *not rich*.

But the ire in his eyes is unyielding. He cocks his head like he's waiting for me to respond.

"Come on, Monroe," he says, and taps my head with his index finger. "I know you didn't have the strongest education growing up, but you aren't dumb, are you?"

I gape at him, speechless.

He averts his eyes like a coward and scoots out of the booth. Shocked and hurt, I watch him walk to the opposite end of the table when I hear the beginning of the Happy Birthday song. I hastily slide out of the booth because I honestly think I might be sick.

How does someone talk to another person with such hatred? Let alone, their girlfriend?

I fling open one of the bathroom stalls and slam the door shut behind me. My entire body shakes with fury, but my mind... My mind shuts down. I sit fully clothed on the toilet, begging my hands to stop shaking, frozen by my mind's cocoon of shame and insecurity.

Tears start to form, then fall. I curl my fingers into fists and squeeze. I squeeze my eyes shut. I squeeze every muscle until my entire body feels like it could crack apart, then I hold my breath.

I make it to fifteen before I'm forced to exhale, and then I suck in a breath and do it again.

And again.

And again.

People come in and out of the bathroom. Some knock on the door of my stall. Voices come and go. I ignore all of them.

Only when I've regained my composure enough to exit the bathroom and extract myself from this damnation of an evening do I stand. I wash my hands with cold water, study my face in the mirror, and give myself a silent pep talk that all I have to do is make it to the front of the restaurant and out the door.

Then, I can fall apart.

I step out into the bustling corridor and flip my hair over my shoulder. I don't need to acknowledge anyone. I just need to leave. But when I reenter the dining room, the long table is empty. Busboys clear plates of half-eaten cake while other members of the waitstaff pull singular tables back into their original positions. Everyone is gone. Maybe this should upset me, but all I feel is overwhelming relief.

I round the area where the party was seated, when I hear, "Miss! Miss! Excuse me, Miss!"

I don't know why I turn around.

"Miss, I'm sorry but the bill."

The waiter who had attended to our table shoves a padded black bill holder at me, and I scrunch my face in confusion, unclear what's happening.

"The bill. No one paid. I don't know where the rest of your party went, but everyone is gone."

My eyes flare wide. Surely, this is a misunderstanding.

"Gone?" I clarify. "They're not just standing outside."

"No," he stiffens. "We checked."

"Unfortunately, if the bill is not paid, we have to call the police."

I blink. "You mean, if I don't pay, you'll have me arrested."

"Well, yes. I'm sorry. But you're the only one left here of your party."

"Umm, okay," I stammer. "I'll pay it, I guess."

I take the bill holder and nervously open it to see the receipt. My brain runs through possible totals for the meal given the amount of people. I scan the slip of paper and see...

Oh my God.

I think I'm going to pass out.

The number is so high that my eyes can't seem to focus.

I can't afford this! I don't even think my credit card has a high enough limit to pay for this! Heat and sweat overtake my senses.

"Sorry. I have to sit. I just need a minute," I say to the waiter as I pull out the nearest chair.

This is a dream. No, a nightmare. This can't be real.

I literally have had dreams like this – of getting a bill for something and not being able to pay. My heart races as adrenaline takes over. I start to claw at my coat because I think I might hyperventilate. I can feel my face getting hotter and hotter. I'm going to go to jail because my entitled prick of a boyfriend and his shitty, wretched friends decided to dine and dash on a six-thousand-dollar bill. And I'll have no one to call. Who would I call? Gabi?

"Monroe?"

I look up at the sound of my name, seconds from a complete breakdown.

"Are you okay?"

Oh God, him? Why him of all people?

Knox pulls out the chair next to me, and I stare wildly at his neatly composed dirty-blonde hair and expertly tailored suit jacket. I can't comprehend that he's here, nor can I form complete sentences. All I can think of is the six-thousand-dollar check I can't pay.

He leans closer, sensing my alarm. "What's wrong? Where's Kieren? Weren't you here for his birthday dinner?"

I nod, but I can't get my breathing under control enough to speak. My shaking hand rests on the closed bill holder. How am I going to pay for this? What am I going to do?

Knox is visibly concerned. "Do you want me to call him?"

I vehemently shake my head.

I open my purse and take out my wallet. Maybe my card will go through. I'll deal with the fallout later. I'll find a way to pay for it. I'll get a full-time job while I'm back in Ohio.

Knox pulls the bill holder away before I can slide my card inside.

He makes a surprised face, but our reactions could not be more different. His surprise is one of amusement. My surprise was one of horror.

He furrows his brows and looks at me. "Why are you paying for this?" he asks. I manage a shrug, holding my credit card between my thumb and middle finger, sensing my lower lip begin to quiver. Am I honestly going to start crying? In public? In front of Knox?

"They all left." I barely get out the words because if I say more, I'll crumble, and so will any remaining dignity.

"I'm sorry, did I hear you correctly? They left and stuck you with the fucking bill?" he asks with angry disbelief.

Tears pool along my lower waterline, and I look away. I look at anyone but him because as soon as I blink, these tears will fall, and I really don't want this perfectly poised, swoon-worthy man to see me cry.

I don't realize Knox has pulled out his wallet until I hear the toss of his credit card against the check holder.

"No, you can't," I stammer. My hand flies out in protest, and those goddamn tears break free.

"Knox, I'm serious," I say, swiping the tears away. "You cannot. Why would you do this? You don't even like him."

He closes the black folder and nods at the waiter hovering nearby, who eagerly rushes over.

"Thank you, sir," the waiter says with earnest gratitude. Having been a waitress myself, I know the hell I would have endured if I'd let a table of fifteen skip out on their bill, even if it wasn't my fault.

My eyes shift away from the waiter's retreating form and back to Knox. In the dim light, I can see the depth in his grey-blue irises. They're soft, steady, and unwavering. It hits me then – who he looks like. With his dirty blonde locks and charming eyes that contrast his stern face, he looks like the lead actor on that crime drama about an outlaw motorcycle gang. All he's missing is the facial hair.

"What's that look?" he asks, with a perplexed grin.

"Nothing. Just... it's nothing," I say with a shy shake of my head.

He reaches up to touch my cheek, and the contact of his fingertips against my skin makes my breath hitch. "The devil doesn't deserve your tears, Monroe," Knox says. "Remember that." Heat flushes my face. His voice is deep and gruff yet smooth and soothing.

I look away, embarrassed to understand that everyone knows Kieren is a piece of shit, and somehow, I'm just now realizing that fucking him does not make me immune to his hatefulness. It's like a cruel joke told at my expense, but I've been laughing along the whole time. Turns out, I'm the joke. I'm the fool who is fucking the asshole.

The waiter returns the bill to Knox for his signature.

"Thank you," I manage. "I'll find a way to pay you back."

"No, you won't," he says, folding the customer copy of the receipt and placing it in his wallet.

"I'm looking forward to humbling that motherfucker next semester when I take over as president," he grins. "So, he'll pay, one way or the other."

"Are you going to make him clean toilets?" I smile.

"That and a lot worse," he winks.

"Well, umm, thank you," I offer uneasily, feeling like I should go. I'm sure Knox is here with friends or even a date and needs to get back to his table.

"So, are you heading out to meet up with all those horrible people?" Knox asks, making no move to stand. I can't tell if he's making polite chit-chat or sincerely wants to prolong our conversation.

"They went to some club in Chelsea, but at this point, I'm just going to leave."

"For the airport?" he asks.

"No. I wish. For the bus station. I have to take the bus back to Dornell to pick up my car, then drive to Ohio."

Knox glances down at the large Rolex watch on his wrist. "It's almost midnight," he comments.

"And?" I ask.

"I doubt there are any buses leaving for Dornell right now. You can't stay the night in the bus terminal, Monroe, it's not safe."

"No! I wasn't planning to sleep in the bus terminal!" I exclaim. "Kieren got a hotel for the night. I'll just go back there and wait it out until morning. I have to get my stuff anyway."

"What's the name of the hotel?"

"The Pendry. Why?"

"What's your last name, Monroe?"

"Campbell, but why?"

Knox levels me a serious look. "Listen, your relationship with Kieren is none of my business, but I'm texting my family's concierge right now to book a room for you. That way, when you get there, the choice is yours."

"Knox, that's..." I shake my head. "That's totally unnecessary. And absurd. You just paid a six-thousand-dollar dinner tab!"

"What does one have to do with the other?" he asks earnestly. "Besides, I'll feel better knowing you have the option. Okay, she just confirmed the booking. Let me call you a car, then I'll walk you out."

"A car? Knox, you really don't need to do all this!" I insist, flustered by his abundant generosity. "Please, go back to your table. Aren't you here with people?"

"It's just my parents, they'll live," he chuckles. "Besides, it's the least I can do."

"The least?" I gape. "But you've already done the absolute most!"

Knox huffs in disagreement as he navigates the car service app on his phone.

"What?" I challenge.

He shakes his head as he sets his phone down. "This is my fault. I let him get to you first," he states, crossing his arms as he holds my gaze. My brows furrow together in confusion.

"The day of the Sigma barbecue," he begins in explanation, "I saw you. I was stuck talking to some insufferable freshman – a senator's grandson whom I was told I needed to meet – when I looked over and saw the most beautiful woman I'd ever seen. But I didn't act fast enough. I kept talking to that idiot, waiting for a pause in conversation to extract myself. I lost sight of you for thirty seconds, and when I found you again, it was too late. Kieren was already there."

A mix of emotions swirls in my mind as I take in Knox's crestfallen expression. His regret is strange but so is contemplating this alternative reality. What would my life be like if he had gotten there first? I hardly know him, he's a step above complete stranger. But from our brief interaction at the alumni mixer, in some ways, he seems very similar to Kieren, but in other ways, he seems starkly different.

Would I have fallen in love with Knox like I've fallen in love with Kieren, despite myself? Despite knowing that Kieren is perhaps not a good person, yet I crave him with a desperation I cannot quench or explain. Would our relationship have had the same intensity? Would he have sexually set me free in the same way Kieren has? I'm not sure the way Kieren makes me feel can be replicated, which is a ruinous truth I'm scared to say aloud.

"Your car's here," Knox comments, pocketing his phone as he stands. "I'll walk you out."

I follow him, silently mulling over my thoughts of this bizarre run-in with Knox at a random restaurant in Manhattan, where he not only saved me from humiliation by paying for Kieren's outrageous birthday dinner, but also booked me a hotel room, because... he cares?

Because, for reasons that make no sense outside of thinking I'm attractive, he may have unresolved feelings? Because Kieren is apparently a blatant monster, evident to everyone, and maybe my concern for my own well-being should be greater than that of a complete fucking stranger? I can't sort through all this.

Nor can I ever tell Kieren that Knox paid for his birthday dinner because his friends left the bill unpaid. It would only backfire against me, and I can't weather a repeat of Kieren's wrath, like what happened after the alumni mixer. I'm sure Kieren assumes his bestie *Helena* paid for the meal, and whatever, might as well let him run with that belief because it's honestly not worth the turmoil.

"It was good to see you again, Monroe. Get home safe, okay?" Knox says as he opens the car door.

"Thank you," I stutter, struggling to express the immense gratitude yet overwhelming guilt I feel. "I don't know what to say. I… I'm sorry."

"For what?" he asks, smirking like my need to apologize is ridiculous.

"That it wasn't you," I admit. My body short-circuits as soon as the words leave my mouth.

Knox glances away in contemplation as he holds the passenger door open. Icy December air whips around us both. Even though I'm seated inside the heated car, I'm frozen because *why did I just say that?*

Finally, his eyes turn back to land on mine. "Who knows?" he says with a surrendering shrug. "Maybe one day, the Universe will give me another chance."

"Happy holidays, Monroe," he says with a sorrowful smile, but before I can echo his well wishes, the door he had held open is suddenly, but not harshly, shut.

17
KIEREN

End of January, Freshman Year,
Dornell University

"Jace, you've been styling your hair for the last twenty fucking minutes," I shout across our room. I gnaw at my bottom lip while tossing a lacrosse ball in the air as I lie on my bed, debating.

"Not my fault you fucked things up with Monroe," Jace responds. I swear to fuck if he doesn't stop primping, I'm throwing this ball at his goddamn head.

"Where are you and Gabs going tonight?" I ask, though I don't give a fuck.

"You mean Gabi?"

"Whatever."

He chuckles as he pulls on a dress shirt. "You're so bitter," Jace comments.

I toss the ball above my head, catching it on the way down before it collides with my face. Of course I'm fucking bitter. I'm bitter that Monroe won't return any of my attempts to contact her, and now that she's joined the best sorority on campus, I'm bitter that I have to listen to every fuck head with a pulse talk about *'the hot blonde pledge in Delta Gamma.'* I swear to God, if one more pencil dick motherfucker calls her '*Marilyn Monroe*' in my presence, he'll lose his tongue.

"I believe she told Gabi it was the worst night of her life," Jace recounts with amusement.

I fling the ball at him, landing a direct hit on the shoulder.

"Ouch, dickhead!" he yells.

"*I know*, Jace," I snarl. "You've only told me what you overheard a thousand times. I don't need to hear it again."

"This is why I don't drink. I turn into a monster," I huff, crossing my arms over my chest. The details of my birthday dinner night back in December are hazy, at best. I remember that I was pissed at Monroe for not coming with me to Switzerland, and I remember feeling angry with her at the start of the night. I know we had an argument, but I couldn't tell you what either of us said. After that, my memory is blank.

Alcohol and certain medications I take don't play nice together. Copious amounts of alcohol combined with narcotics, which I don't remember doing, but Barrett informed me the next day I did enough cocaine to kill a horse, are a recipe for disaster.

I woke up face down on my hotel room bed, fully clothed, at noon the next day. When I checked my phone, I saw multiple outgoing calls and texts to Monroe around five-thirty in the morning, which I assume is when I returned to the hotel.

"Pretty sure you're a monster even when you're sober," Jace says, fastening the last button of his shirt.

"Yeah, but I'm better at controlling myself when I'm not drunk and high."

"How are you going to survive the rest of this semester at

Sigma? Or the next three years for that matter? The hazing has just gotten started, and you know it's only going to get worse."

"God, Knox is such a fucking bitch," I grumble.

"That guy is a nightmare. And he clearly has it out for you," Jace jests.

"Just wait until I take the reins as president. I'll be so much worse. You know I expect you to be my number two, right? We need to restore this pussy-ass fraternity to power," I say, my tone serious.

Jace scoffs. "Whatever, man. Power is your thing, not mine."

I sit up, because that comment burrows under my skin like a goddamn tick, and if I have to resort to extreme measures to get him to fall in line, I will.

"Jace, we've talked about this. You and me. We've had this conversation about restoring Sigma to what it once was numerous times. You're not going to reneg on your promise over some pussy, are you?"

When he doesn't answer, I remind him, "Power over pussy, Jace."

He shakes his head like my words are a fucking joke.

"Speaking of pussy, I need to go," he says dismissively, reaching for his coat. I spring off my bed, debate settled. "I'm coming with you."

"No," he protests. "Gabi will kill me."

I shrug, pulling on my winter coat. "Sounds like a you problem. But don't worry, I'll come to your funeral."

"Hey! NO!" Gabi snaps when her eyes find me standing beside Jace in the hallway. "What the fuck is he doing here?" she hisses.

"Nice to see you too, Gabs," I deadpan. "Is Monroe in there?"

She slams the door shut, but their voices can still be heard from the hallway.

Gabi swings open the door, wearing a pissed off look. She gives me a hateful glare before turning to Jace. "I am so fucking mad at you right now," she spits at him. I try to contain my grin because I see she's gripping her coat and ready to leave.

I side-step around her to find Monroe sitting cross-legged on her bed with a laptop open in front of her. She looks at me with an empty expression, and the absence of emotion throws me off-kilter. Anger I can work with. Anger is encouraging. Ambivalence is terrifying.

"Monroe, call me if you need me to come back early," Gabi grouses before leveling a final threatening glance in my direction and closing the door.

Thirty seconds of tense silence pass before Monroe acknowledges my presence.

"Why are you here, Kieren?" Monroe asks without glancing up at me from her laptop.

I cock my head, readying for battle. "Because I've called and texted you ad nauseam for the last month and a half, but you won't fucking talk to me."

"I'm not sure why you think I'd want to talk to you," she responds as she types.

I close the short distance between us and snap that fucking laptop shut. She doesn't even look surprised. I resist the urge to fling it across the room and set it on the floor instead.

"I don't give a fuck if you want to talk to me or not. I'm here now, and we're going to fucking talk." I kick off my shoes and plop onto her bed. Neither of us speaks, so I decide to start with the obvious.

"What happened the night of my birthday dinner?"

"*What happened?*" she gapes.

"I don't remember anything other than waking up the next morning, and you were gone."

"Did you fuck Helena?" she asks.

"What? No! Why would I fuck Helena?"

Monroe stares at me like she's contemplating gouging my eyes out.

"Well, let's see," she begins. "The reservation was in her name, she was flirting with you the entire dinner, she brought a birthday cake to the restaurant, and you invited her to join your ski trip."

"Oh, and, *and*," Monroe pauses for emphasis, "you basically broke up with me at the table, and when I came out of the restroom, you and the entire group were gone."

"I broke up with you?" I shoot back in disbelief. "No, that didn't happen."

"Are you gaslighting me, because you can get the fuck out," she snaps, pointing to the door.

I run my hand over my face with a groan. "What did I say?" I ask.

"I'm not repeating it," she scowls.

"Okay, well that's not fair. Monroe, just tell..."

"I *said* I'm not repeating it. You know, my mom has said some fucked up shit to me over the years, Kieren, but even she hasn't stooped so low. I get it. Someone like me, with my humble upbringing and lack of wealth, will never be good enough for you. I knew it was true. I felt it deep down. I was a fool to think you might actually have feelings for me. You're embarrassed and repulsed by me, which is so fucking shitty because do you think I chose to grow up the way I did? Do you think I wanted that life? Do you think I like being broke and inferior in a sea of rich fucking assholes like you? *And...*," she begins, but stops herself.

"And what?" I push, wondering how there could possibly be more.

She pauses, like she wants to say something, but just shakes her head.

I watch her pretty face turn an angry shade of crimson. Tears fall from her eyes after berating me with a gumption I've not heard before. The bitches in her sorority must be rubbing off on her, and as much as her diatribe irks me, I know I need to tread carefully to regain the upper hand.

"Monroe, in no world am I repulsed..."

"You were terrible to me, Kieren," she cuts me off, swiping at her tears in frustration. "So please, get off my bed and fucking leave."

"I'm not leaving," I state with resolve, reaching to wipe away a stray tear rolling down her cheek. "I'm sorry you're hurt, but I promise you, I honestly do not remember."

"Being drunk is not an excuse."

"Okay!" I say in placation. "Again, I'm sorry."

Our argument falls quiet, both of us debating our next move.

"Will you give me another chance?" I ask, ending the standoff.

She refuses to look at me, but we've been here before – same emotions, same bed.

Scooting closer, I cup her face with my hand, skimming her bottom lip with my thumb.

"Kiss me," I rasp against her hair, but she refuses. "Fucking kiss me, Monroe," I beg through clenched teeth. My desperation to taste her grows primal, my raw plea hangs in the air unanswered, and I feel my tether to sanity begin to unravel. I can't control myself around this woman. The sheer proximity of her ignites an obsessive fire I can't put out.

She whimpers as I kiss the side of her face, descending

down her jawline and neck. I feel her body slacken and leverage this moment of surrender to pull her onto my lap. Her lips barely part when I kiss them, but it's all the give I need to shove my tongue inside her mouth and taste her. *Fuck, this woman.*

Suddenly, she pulls back. "Stop Kieren!" she pleads. Her head wants me to stop, but I guarantee her pussy is begging for me to continue. I release her mouth but refuse to free her from my embrace.

"I know you say you don't remember, but the way you treated me that night was deplorable. What you said was beyond hurtful. I cried myself to sleep for weeks."

Tears fall from her eyes as she covers her face with her hands. A sob shakes free when I tighten my arms around her. I'm losing this fight. I'm losing miserably.

"Tell me what I have to do to make this right. I'll do anything," I implore.

"You told me you didn't want a future together," she cries.

"I truly don't remember saying such a thing, but I was drunk, Monroe, and angry. I was angry you didn't choose me."

"What are you talking about?" she sniffs indignantly.

"You didn't choose to spend the holidays with me."

"Kieren, that's not fair. You know my situation. You can't make me choose between you and my grandmother. She's all the family I have."

My jaw clenches in frustration because she doesn't fucking get it.

"You were supposed to be mine, Monroe," I remind her. "*My* girlfriend. You should have wanted to spend the holidays *with me*. I offered a thousand times to pay so you could come on the trip. I would have paid for your flight back to Ohio as well if you had just asked."

"Is something else going on?" I push. "Is this because

you're in a sorority now and you want to see other people? Have you met someone else?"

My heart beats with fear. I can't handle her leaving me. Even the possibility of her abandonment makes me feel out of control.

"Monroe," I begin, dangerously teetering on the edge. "Is there someone else?"

"No," she answers, and thank God. Thank fucking God. I thought I was going to have to kill someone tonight.

I swallow, knowing what I must say to call her mine once more. "Listen, I don't know what this is between us, or how to label it, but I do have feelings for you, Monroe. Very intense feelings. I need you in a way I've never needed anyone before, but I don't know how to love you right now. Not in the way you want and also not when the Sigma pledge process is just beginning."

"But I can't let you go," I continue. "You're mine Monroe. I've claimed you, remember? And I know this semester will be a shit show, but I'm going to lose my fucking mind if you're not in my bed every night. The thought of you roaming around, guys hitting on you, trying to fuck you... I can't Monroe. I can barely think it, let alone say it out loud." My voice is raw and broken, and despite my intentional effort to overindex on vulnerability, I don't think this is entirely an act.

"I'm scared to let you back in," she admits. I stroke her silky strands of hair, debating the right words to say. She's not wrong to feel this way, as infuriating as that is to admit. The deeper I get into the Sigma pledge process, the more my monster will be on full display. Excessive drinking is unavoidable, and I fear what I might say or do when under the influence.

But I know one thing for certain. My behavior will be

unhinged in the worst of ways if she's not mine. I need to win her back, even at the expense of my pride.

"I know," I agree at last. "I don't deserve you, but please, Monroe. I am begging you. Please, one more chance."

She sighs. "Maybe," she concedes. "Gabi's going to kill me."

"We should probably leave then," I say, gripping the base of her hair to tilt her head back so my lips can find hers. She moans against my mouth as our kisses build with hunger. Goddamn, I want to fuck her. I want to throw her down on this tiny twin bed and fuck her into next week.

"I've missed you so fucking much Monroe," I groan, my greedy hands palming every inch of her. "Please be mine. Please tell me how much you missed me, that you want me."

"Promise me you'll do better, Kieren," she presses, breathy with need as she rocks her pelvis against my now stiffening groin.

"For you, Monroe, I'll try," I offer, unsure why I picked this moment of all moments to be honest, but it doesn't seem to matter. The answer is sufficient enough, and our temporary setback is over. She's mine again, and since I know she has needs only I can fulfill, I'll make sure she stays mine, from now until my dying day.

18
MONROE

Beginning of Summer Break Between Freshman and Sophomore Year, Ohio

I don't know how to do this.

I suck in a sob as I look around my grandmother's house. Rotten food, unwashed dishes, stacks of papers everywhere... After returning to Dornell in January, I was so caught up with sorority stuff and school work and just fucking living my life for once, that I didn't come back to Ohio to visit during the spring like I promised.

My poor grandmother.

I didn't realize her health had gotten so bad.

This is my fault.

And a funeral, a casket, a headstone – I couldn't pay for any of it. I could barely afford to have her cremated.

This wasn't supposed to happen. I was supposed to live

with Gabi and two other girls from our sorority over the summer in New York City. I had a waitressing job lined up. The other girls all had summer internships thanks to family connections, although none of them sounded particularly legitimate. Someone's uncle or aunt or mom or dad called in a favor, and suddenly, a summer internship doing administrative work at so-and-so's hedge fund or law firm or startup magically appeared. I'm not even sure these internships are paid, but what did they care? They didn't need to make money. Was I envious? Yes, but I was content to work my waitressing job until I figured out something better.

And Kieren...

Fucking Kieren.

Interning at his family's wealth management company, which one day will become his legacy. Everything he is has been handed to him on a silver fucking platter. Kieren and I were together most of last semester, but right now, I can't stand to look at him.

He's... changed. My relationship with Kieren imploded right after finals when an anonymous number texted Gabi a video of Jace getting his dick sucked by a girl neither of us knew, which was bad enough until we got to the part of the video where she climbed onto his lap and fucked him. I'm convinced Kieren sent the video, but he pretended to be clueless when I confronted him. Gabi said the source didn't matter. It didn't change the fact that Jace cheated. I suppose she's right.

I've never seen a man beg like Jace begged for Gabi. He got on his knees and sobbed, pleading with her not to break up with him. I tried to leave the room because it was so fucking uncomfortable, but Gabi wouldn't let me.

But damn do I wish I had her resolve. She refused to tell him about the video. Instead, she said she wanted to be single.

She wanted to go into the summer unattached, and while it had been fun, she didn't want to be tied down.

I watched two hearts break that day.

But I have to give Gabi credit, because while I know she's barely holding it together, on the outside, she looks like she's never been better. She says she plans to live her best life this summer, and I believe her.

Me, on the other hand. I made it all of three days in New York City before I got the phone call. When forty-eight hours passed and I couldn't get in touch with my grandmother to tell her about the adventures I'd had so far in Manhattan, I asked a neighbor to do a wellness check. When my grandmother didn't answer after ten minutes of knocking, the neighbor walked around to the back of the house and found an unlocked door and my grandmother's crumpled, decaying body in an armchair by the television.

They told me it was a stroke, and that she didn't suffer, but how the fuck would they know? No amount of assurances will ever ease my guilt.

They tried to call my mom, but of course, she's incarcerated, so I'm the only viable next of kin. I spent nearly all my savings on a plane ticket and rental car.

And, now I'm here.

Alone.

Gabi offered to come with me, but I didn't want to ruin the start of her summer.

When I got the news about my grandmother, I almost called Kieren. Hardly a day goes by that he doesn't call or text, desperately trying to see me and claiming he didn't send the video. I'm sure he would have loved to get the call, especially at a time when I'm feeling vulnerable and broken. He'll inevitably get the news about my grandmother at some point and probably insist on flying out to Ohio to see me.

Although, the thought of Kieren Hunt setting foot in rural Ohio is a comedy worth watching.

I wish I could say I don't still have feelings for him, but fuck, he ruined me, and deep down I know our reconciliation is inevitable. No one has ever made me feel so alive and yet so devastated at the same time. I secretly yearn for him in a way I can't, for the life of me, understand, and I find myself obsessing over all the ways he used to touch me.

What the actual fuck is wrong with me? I would give anything to go back to those first few months of freshman year, before everything went to shit. And the fucked up thing is those months weren't even that great, but I can't stop wanting him, and it's destroying me. My memories of him, of us together, eat at my insides like a slow-moving cancer.

I walk over to the nearest window and wrestle the stubborn wooden frame to get it open. I've been in Ohio for a week and done fuck all other than move the armchair to the curb and collect my grandmother's ashes. Even with the armchair outside, the house still reeks of death, but I've been too exhausted to clean. Sleeping has been impossible because I've convinced myself that every little noise I hear is the ghost of my grandmother haunting this place. It's probably just the cockroaches and mice, but knowing the walls are teeming with vermin is an even less comforting thought.

Standing in the center of the living room, I break down. My grandmother left this house to me. I know I need to sell it because not only do I need the money, but I can't afford the mortgage. But how do you sell a house? I'm fucking nineteen. I have no idea what I'm doing. The process alone feels daunting, and right now, I'm so riddled with grief and guilt that I can barely function.

I know I have a limited window of time before I default on

the mortgage and the bank repossesses the house, but the excruciating reality of my situation is crippling.

A sob rips up my throat, because how?

How am I going to get through this?

It's been three hours since my breakdown, but I've managed to fill five trash bags. Even though it's barely a dent and the house is still covered in filth, it's something.

A loud knock rattles the screen door. Fuck, it's probably the neighbor again. She's friendly but I wish she'd leave me the fuck alone and let me sort through the scraps of my grandmother's delirium in peace.

Wiping the sweat from my forehead, I draw a steadying breath and brace myself.

"Hi... oh my God," I stammer.

"Surprise!"

I can't move, my body frozen, but that doesn't stop the tears from falling.

"Gabi, you don't say *'surprise'* to someone who just lost a family member," the woman standing next to Gabi scolds.

"Monroe, we're so sorry for your loss. I'm Gabi's Mom. She always talks about you, and I wish we were meeting for the first time under different circumstances."

"Jesus, Monroe," Gabi gawks, looking at the mess behind me. Mess is an understatement. I turn around as if I don't know the horror that lies within.

"It's really bad," I cry, my body shaking.

Gabi's mom pulls me in for a hug, and Gabi wraps her arms around me from behind.

"You're not alone, Monroe," Gabi says to comfort me. "We came to help you."

"And I don't know if Gabi has told you, but I'm a real estate agent. I'm not licensed in Ohio, but I'll hold your hand through the process and make sure no one takes advantage of you."

"Thank you," I sob. We stand huddled together until my sobs subside and I can form coherent sentences.

"Have you been staying in there?" Gabi asks, concerned.

"Where else would I stay?"

"Monroe," Gabi says with a pitying look.

Her mom steps inside, immediately covering her nose. I watch her curiously, but she doesn't balk.

"Okay," she says after a long look around. "Monroe, grab your things. You're going to stay with us. We've got a hotel about thirty minutes from here. Let's have dinner, get a good night of sleep, and start fresh tomorrow. It's a lot of work, but not impossible. I'll find a professional cleaning company to help us."

"I… I can't afford that," I admit.

"I'll front you the money. We can figure it out after the sale," she says.

"But, you'll let me pay you back, right?"

The kindest smile I've ever seen crosses her face. "Let's just pretend I'm saying yes."

"Mrs. Pimentel, I can't…"

"Monroe, listen," Gabi cuts in. "One day, it'll be your turn to be the hero, but that day is not today, okay? Now turn around, get your shit, and let's go."

I press my lips together to stop their quivering, but it's no use.

"Gabi, I love you," I manage. My hoarse voice cracks from days spent crying.

She puts her hand on my heart and then takes my hand in hers, pressing my palm to her chest. Her heart beats under my skin, as mine does to hers. Two friends, two hearts, together.

"Ride or die, Monroe," she says, scanning my eyes with unwavering certainty.

"Ride or fucking die, Gabi," I whisper in return as a warm feeling spreads across my body, and I realize something profound.

I am not alone, but more than that, I am *loved.*

BONUS CHAPTER

SPOILERS WITHIN!

Do not read unless you've read Caged,
Book 1 of the Sins of the Sigma Series.
Proceed With Caution.

19
BONUS CHAPTER: KIEREN'S POV

(This is an alternate POV of Chapters 1 & 43 in Book 1, Caged)

The Night Monroe Escaped, Second Semester (April), Junior Year, Sigma

The hint of dissention lingers on my palate as I stumble tipsy and high through the hall on my way back to my sweet puppy. Huddled whispers, sideways glances lasting just a bit too long, unsettled nerves, but not fear – a concern I'll need to rectify.

Because fear is the only weapon I have to wield.

Survival is intrinsic to our reptilian brain. I'm no fool to think these women will willingly offer themselves as a sacrifice to the higher power like the ancient, lost texts of the Sigma Charter claim happened a century prior.

Today's Sigma isn't a cult, despite all the work I've put into rebuilding our reputation and traditions this past semester.

How am I going to keep this charade afloat for the rest of this year and next? And once I graduate, how does Sigma keep the Ritual of Sacrifice alive without drawing suspicion at some point? Yes, women go missing all the time, but one every month during the academic year risks a visit from the FBI, who might become convinced a serial killer is on the loose.

Was this really not an issue in my grandfather's day and age? I guess times were different then.

Women didn't have the same career opportunities as men, and convincing a woman to become a Sigma Sinner and pledge herself in service to The Brotherhood for the promise of a husband was a more straightforward proposition. And not just any husband. A Sigma. You'd guarantee yourself a comfortable future, and all you had to do was spread your legs. But you also might die. A high-stakes gamble, but worth the price of admission.

Would the women downstairs at the mixer tonight die for the promise of a husband who could provide future wealth and security? Fuck no, which is why the longevity of continuing the Ritual of Sacrifice at Dornell's Sigma chapter seems fucked, but I suppose I'll have to find a way if I'm to graduate to my father's satisfaction. *Fuck that motherfucker.*

Perhaps I'm underestimating my ability to turn Sigma into the cult it once was half a century ago. Perhaps I'm projecting Monroe's doubt onto myself. No one ran away after her little outburst a few days ago at the Full Moon Ceremony. In fact, the congregation of heathens looked at her like she'd lost her mind. She screamed for them to run, but no one moved a fucking inch.

Maybe the whispers tonight are my own paranoia.

I know I'm not in my right mind.

The safety tether anchoring me to the spacecraft that is my sanity has irreparably snapped, and I'm floating away into the dark abyss of psychosis.

I know this, and yet I keep going, unchanged and out of control.

I need to stop myself, but I can't.

I've had Monroe in a fucking dog cage for the past two days, for fuck's sake. Or has it been three? *Fuck!* I scream into my mind's void.

I'm furious with her, but that's not why I've yet to release her. I'm well aware I'm keeping her caged for my own sick comfort at this point. She's there because possessing her in this way means she can't run, can't leave, can't *abandon me.*

Am I really going to kill her as X demands?

Of course I am.

But will I?

Jace is right. I should give my puppy fresh food and water. A bath. Snuggles. I should hold her, pet her, please her, but I don't trust myself. Every minute of indulgence, of allowing myself to love her, will be marred by the relentless whispers of that fucking demon on my shoulder telling me I should *snap her neck.*

But who is the demon?

Is it X, my father, Sigma?

Or, is it me?

I fear I know the answer, which is why I can't let myself love her. *But fuck, I love her so fucking much.* I know she's not a pet I can keep, but I can't go on like this.

I can't keep telling myself that I hate her, that she disgusts me, while admiring my possession like a rare, exotic animal kept behind glass. I am *unraveling.* I sense my cognizance disintegrating, devolving into madness, yet there is nothing I can do to stop the forward motion of the train – a train where I am but a mere passenger. It's ironic how I can control the minds of those around me, yet the one mind I cease to control is my own.

My little secret.

I twist my key into the three deadbolt locks securing my bedroom, weary from my own warring thoughts.

The door swings open and...

I blink, swaying and unsteady, rendered immobile by stunned panic. It's like I'm watching the end of the Earth unfold in slow motion; an asteroid, a thousand-foot mega-tsunami, an alien invasion, a catastrophe so colossal that it can't be real. My head floats above my body, processing the end of me.

My mind cannot comprehend the truth my eyes see.

"Monroe?" I call, finding my voice. She might be in the bathroom. A logical location.

My feet carry me the few steps it takes to reach the bathroom door, left partially ajar with the light on. Cautiously, I push it fully open. The beat of my heart pounds in my throat as I pull back the shower curtain.

"Monroe?" I call again, sharply this time, as I hastily scramble back into the bedroom. My steps feel jerky and uneven from adrenaline, my breaths choppy and shallow.

I stand, stupefied and alone in the middle of the room, and then, I feel it...

A scant breeze puffs against the skin of my face. The curtain subtly flutters. The window is... open?

How?

The window that has probably been sealed shut for fucking decades is OPEN?!

How did I miss it?

Sprinting over to the window, my fingers wrap around the

jagged and scratched sill. Ridges of scraped paint press against my palm.

How long?

How long has she been planning this?

I did this. I left her in here, unguarded, for an entire week. She...

She's been planning this since spring break.

Devastation crashes into me as I grasp my own error while simultaneously realizing how calculated she has been. Her hatred for me... *When she fucked me mere days ago.* She *used me* like she always *uses me!*

My frantic vision bounces between the night sky and her empty cage.

She ESCAPED!

Rage and despair mingle underneath my skin.

She RAN!

Fury rips from my lips in the form of her name as I scream into the empty, black horizon.

My fucking puppy, my puppy, my puppy, my puppy, I swirl, spinning, dizzy, gasping.

I can't breathe, I can't see, I can't!

Dropping to my knees, I claw at my chest like a suicidal maniac determined to rip out his own heart. Maybe I can find her. Maybe it's not too late.

But I know the truth. My beautiful, perfect pet. My love...

She's gone.

TO BE CONTINUED

THIS CONCLUDES THE PREQUEL NOVELLA

Jump into the rest of the Sins of the Sigma Series here or find it on Amazon and Kindle Unlimited.

Fear not, sweet puppy.

The story of Kieren and Monroe is far from over.

ABOUT THE AUTHOR

Summer Robert is a recovering corporate girlie turned weaver of angsty, dark romance stories that are as suspenseful as they are salacious. After leaving the corporate world behind, Summer published her debut dark romance series, GOOD HURT, and hopes she can continue to delight and captivate the reader community with her twisted and often emotionally devastating love stories, unhinged spice, and gut-wrenching cliffhangers. Summer loves a good Easter egg written between the pages as much as she loves surviving off of caffeine and vibes. And if you're looking for Easter eggs, given Summer is a hoarder and self-proclaimed connoisseur of perfume, the fragrance worn by the main characters might be a good place to start.

Most importantly, she's a mom of two small humans and one small, vicious, and spiteful yorkipoo. Summer currently resides in Los Angeles, and although she is originally a native Ohioan from a shockingly small farm town, she will forever call LA her home.

Follow Summer on social media for unhinged and entertaining posts about her books and characters, as well as book news and announcements. For behind-the-scenes goodies, lost chapters, and to dive deeper into Summer's books, join her newsletter.

TT: https://www.tiktok.com/@summerrobertwrites

IG: https://www.instagram.com/summerrobertwrites/

Website (Buy Signed Copies & Merch):
www.summerrobert.com

Follow Summer on Amazon

Join Summer's Newsletter

www.ingramcontent.com/pod-product-compliance
Lightning Source LLC
LaVergne TN
LVHW010659110826
845149LV00014B/3171

* 9 7 9 8 9 9 8 5 2 3 9 9 1 *